THE HERO'S SON

Laia Losantos

This is a work of fiction. Unless otherwise indicated, all the names, characters, businesses, places, events and incidents in this book are either the product of the author's imagination or used in a fictitious manner. Any resemblance to actual persons, living or dead, or actual events is purely coincidental.

This book or any portion thereof may not be reproduced or used in any manner whatsoever without the express written permission of the published expect for the use of brief quotations in a book review.

Copyright © 2021 by Laia Losantos – All rights reserved.
ISBN: 9798730816459.
Cover art by Jorge Mendizábal.

Author email: laia_losantos@hotmail.com

To my father.

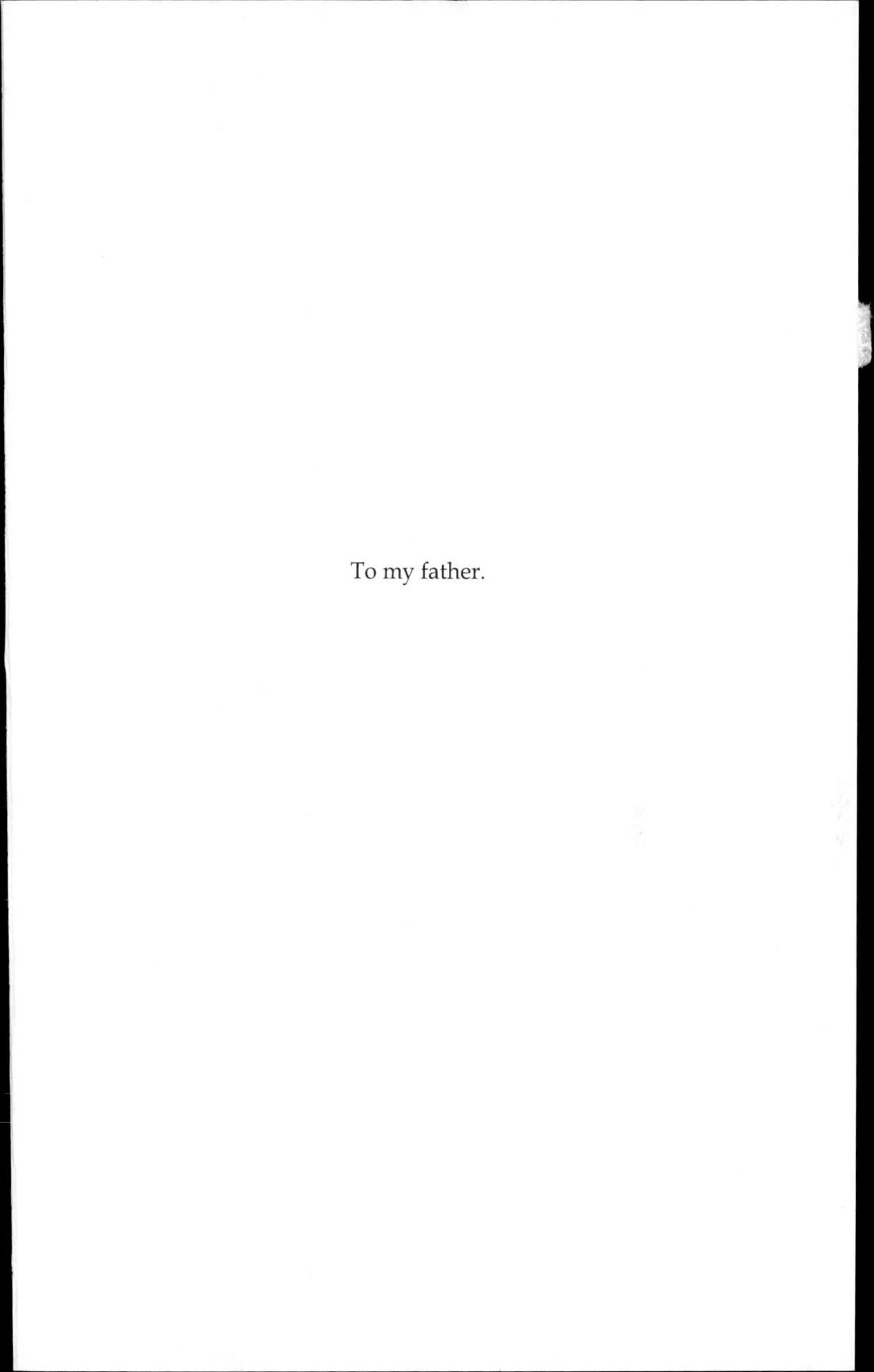

I

After killing with arrows the two slaves and the mule, the bandits abandon their hideouts on the hill. They are eight. They approach the carriage quietly, their guard lowered. The job is done. Now they'll take their bounty and throw the corpses and the carriage down the slope, a bit further on the path.

That's how I found this spot: I literally bumped into a pile of cadavers. In summer, the smell of rotten flesh is sweet and strong.

Today there's something new, though. There is a woman under the carriage. As soon as the first arrows hit the mule, she sought refuge there. That was a smart move. But they have seen her. One of them scares her away from one side, while another one grabs her legs from the other side and pulls her out. Suddenly, she is surrounded by three burly men, who push her away from the carriage. The woman looks at her captors with disgust.

One of them (the leader?) tears off her robe. She has big breasts. Two men pin her legs and arms to the floor, while the leader takes out his dick. The woman fights wildly, but doesn't scream. She just stares at the leader, right in the eye. Four other men stand nearby, enjoying the show from a distance. The remaining bandit is on the carriage, going through the contents of a trunk. It's time to act.

Suddenly I feel a pang of panic. They're eight! They'll see me as soon as I abandon my spot. And then, what? How on Earth am I going to fight eight trained men? As soon as I attack one, the other seven will pierce my chest. I can hear my heart beating strongly, I feel like drowning. Couldn't I keep lying on the dry grass?

A few meters away, to my left, the Harpy stares at me, a tiny human face stuck to a crow's body. I try to hold her gaze, but I can't. I can't.

The Harpy speaks:
Coward.

My first arrow pierces the head of the man sacking the carriage. He drops over the trunk. No one notices: everyone is watching the leader trying to penetrate the naked woman. One of them, a tall guy, caresses his crotch, a silly smile on his face.

My second arrow passes cleanly through his head. The two guys next to him have noticed something, but it's already too late. My next arrows kills the leader, who drops dead over the woman.

Five to go.

They act fast (military training?): before I can set the next arrow, they are all crouched behind the carriage. They already know where I am, so there's no point in hiding any more. With the arrow still in my bow, I stand up and run towards the carriage.

Soon I see the archer standing behind the carriage, his bow ready to shoot. I run in Ss, using the random pattern that my father taught me: left-left-right-right-left-right-left. Two arrows get very close. He's skilled, but didn't get the pattern in time. I'm already in front of the carriage.

Time for acrobatics. I jump on the carriage and follow with a forward flip. While my body is upside-down, I shoot the archer on the face.

Four to go.

I land on my heels on the hard floor, at barely half a meter from the huddled men. Five is multitude, so, without further ado, I drop the bow and start running down the hill. The archer is dead, so I can run straight.

Soon I hear footsteps behind me: one of them is getting close. I allow him to get even closer: if he extended his arm, he could almost touch me... Abruptly, I jump ahead a few meters. The bandit behind me doesn't jump, though, and so falls into my trap: a deep hole covered with leaves, with wooden spikes at the bottom. I hear him gulping for air; then, a thud. If he's dead, he can consider himself lucky.

Three to go.

I run some meters further and look behind. The other three bandits are standing in front of the pit, looking horrified. They are a heavyset unarmed man with black beard, a man carrying an axe and a guy with a helmet. Soon their attention turns back to me.

They chase me for quite a while, at some point we're running up a hill. The landscape has changed: now the ground is pure rock. I run further up and enter a small cave. The bandits follow through.

The cave's walls are very narrow, I could not extend my arms if I wanted to. Light coming from a crack on the cave's ceiling creates a pleasant semi-darkness. The air is humid and cool, but not cold. I reach the end of the cave and turn to face my pursuers.

They enter the cave single file. The first in line is the guy with the helmet, he's drawn out his sword. The other two remain behind, squeezed against the cave's walls.

That's why I chose this place to end the game: if they want a piece of me, they'll have to come one by one.

The guy with the helmet says:

"Leave him to me."

The heavyset one peeps at me from behind the ax guy. He says:

"But... he is a kid!"

I draw my sword and tack the guy with the helmet.

II

I abandon the cave covered with their blood. I am very excited, my legs are shaking. On my left hand, I carry my broken sword: I fought so viciously with the first two bandits, that the blade came off the hilt. The heavyset bandit didn't dare attack me. By the time I finished the other two, he was trying to squeeze himself out of the cave. I killed him with my hands.

I lie on the rock floor and cry.

After a few minutes, I get a grip on myself. I'm breathing heavily, but I'm not sobbing anymore. I can hear water running. I look around and discover the source of a small stream near the cave entrance.

I wash my head and arms in the stream. The water feels fresh, but not cold. Aside from the running water and a few occasional tweets, everything is silent. The sun projects a very pleasant shade where I am squatting. I feel very, very tired.

I walk back to the carriage. When I arrive, the old woman is digging a hole beside the road. She has chosen an unusually soft spot and is using a slate to open the ground. She's wearing a new white dress.

"Are you all right?", I ask.

She turns to me. She is about forty. She isn't pretty, but has very elegant features: high forehead, straight nose, small mouth. She looks into my eyes with confidence. Her gaze is serious and focused.

"Yes, I am fine." She points at a rock. "Please take that slate and help me dig two graves." And she keeps digging.

"For the bandits?"

"For my slaves".

"What for?".

She stops and stares at me. "These two beautiful young boys have served my temple since they were five years old. They were always loyal to me and have died for my sake. I'm not letting them rot in the sun. Now pick up that slate and dig."

I can't think of any reply, so I give in.

By the time we finish, the sun is setting. I pick up the corpse of each slave and leave it gently in the grave.

The woman closes her slaves' eyelids and places a coin under their tongues. She looks at them for a minute and then kisses them on the back of the hand. She stands up.

"Soon it will be cold, we need to make a fire. I'm collecting some twigs. Could you please cover my boys?"

I do as I'm told. She goes far away to fetch that fodder, but I can hear her crying nonetheless.

When she comes back, she is again composed. The woman drops the twigs in front of the graves.

"I need to collect my things", I say. "I come back soon."

She doesn't reply. I go back to my hiding site and pick up my arrows, my sleeping mat and my bag of supplies. The sky is dark-blue, and my hands look like shadows. When I return to the carriage, the wood is already burning.

Soon the woman is sitting on a blanket in front of the fire, contemplating the two graves. She invites me to sit beside her. She offers me wine. I take it: all of a sudden, my throat feels dry like sand. The woman starts roasting some dried meat.

"Thanks for saving my life", she says.

"You're welcome."

"You were not traveling the road, were you?"

I shake my head.

"You were waiting for the gang."

I nod.

"Is that what you do? You kill bandits?"

"Lately."

"Where do you come from?"

"Tyria". I elaborate: "a little village close to Thebes."

"We are far from Thebes."

"I started hunting gangs near my home. When I ran out of them, I started looking elsewhere. I've been ambling around for some weeks."

"Where did you learn to fight?"

I am silent for a while. Finally, I say:

"My father taught me."

"Is he a soldier?"

"No."

She seems amused. "You don't speak much, do you?", she says. I shrug my shoulders. "What is your name, boy?"

"I am Thessalus, son of Thasus."

"Thasus! Do you mean...?"

I nod.

Of course she's heard of him, everyone has. On the pediment of the council house of Eleusis the traveler can still find the relief that countless sculptors have imitated since. My father, the young hero, depicted as a muscled bearded man wearing a winged yellow helmet and an armor. He holds a short double-edged sword. Behind him lies the giant snake of Megara, tied to a large rock. At his feet, a pile of dead warriors. My father, the great Thasus. The man who defeated the Barbarians from the East, the man who tamed a pegasus. The man who dared to fight the god of War and lived to see another day.

After sharing her salted meat with me, the woman seems lost in her thoughts.

"I met your father a long time ago."

I am surprised. "Really? Did he also save your life?"

She laughs. "No. In fact, I got him out of trouble."

"What trouble?"

"Some trouble, never mind. Tell me, Thessalus, what became of your father? I heard that the god Zeus brought Thasus up to the skies and made him a star. That star over there, in fact. Is that your father, Thessalus?"

I didn't notice, but the sky is suddenly black like coal, and full of stars. The woman is pointing at a very bright one, just on top of us.

I look at the star for some seconds. It is large and radiant. But it is alone: there are no other stars next to it. If my father were a star, he would definitely be that one.

"No", I say finally. "My father never raised to the sky. That must have been some other Thasus."

"Sorry. So many rumors, so many versions. Sometimes it is difficult to keep track… Did you know that the stars are still in the sky? It is us who are moving!"

"What…!?"

"That rumor came from Alexandria. And the rumor goes on: all stars are like the sun, but they are so far, far away, that they look like pearls in the sky. Can you imagine?"

We stay silent for a while.

"Where were you going?", I ask.

"My slaves and I were traveling back to my temple in Pallene", she replies.

So she's a priestess. That explains why she's so wise and eloquent.

"I guess that now I'll have to travel alone", she adds.

"If you wish, I will accompany you."

I don't know why I say that. I don't know this woman, why should I care about her fate? But there is something oddly familiar about the Priestess, and I want to stay with her some more time. Somehow, I feel calm and safe by her side.

"Well, that is so gentle of you, young man! There are lots of dangers out there for a woman traveling alone… I accept with grace your generous offer. Now let's sleep, Thessalus. We're waking up at dawn."

The Priestess curls up on the blanket and closes her eyes. Soon she breathes very slowly. She looks relaxed, despite today's events.

I cover my body with my sleeping mat and, using my bag as a pillow, lie on my side, looking at the bonfire.

I think of Mum, I wonder what she's doing now. Probably sitting outside our home, drinking an infusion and breathing the night air. I wonder if she is thinking of me.

III

My grandfather was Antiochus, the king of Pleuron, a small demos in the West. For many years, he and my grandmother Pyrene had been trying to conceive an heir. One day, the king lost his senses, and, in front of everyone, accused Pyrene of murdering her fetuses.

Outraged, a crying Pyrene ran out of the palace and into the forest. She was so mad at her husband! She ran and ran, until she arrived at a beautiful stream. The tall firs cast a delicious shade over the waters, which flowed over a brown rock floor. On the shore, big grey stones grew bright lichen. The soil behind them, covered with moss and rotten fir needles, was exquisitely soft.

But the queen was not alone. Bathing in the stream, there was the most handsome man that she had ever seen. He was very tall and muscled, his skin pale as snow. The dark-haired giant took notice of the queen and smiled. Leaving the water, he walked towards Pyrene and took her hand. The queen hesitated for a moment, then let the man have his way. That man was the god Apollo.

Nine months later, my father was born.

My father was not as handsome as Apollo, but he was an unusual baby nonetheless. In a few weeks he became extraordinarily strong, to the point that the queen could no longer breastfeed him. After several wet nurses quitted their jobs, Antiochus proposed to have his son suck milk directly from Io, the largest cow in the royal stables. And so the baby spent the first year of his life sleeping, drinking milk and playing strength games with the cow.

My father was a very violent toddler. When he got angry, anyone nearby risked his life! At age three, he killed his music teacher because he corrected him on a note on the lyre. Since no one dared discipline him, my father quickly became a spoiled brat. He would fill up a well with rocks, hug a horse till suffocation, demolish a house in order to kill a fly... As a young child, he was already regarded as a public enemy. What would he do when he reached puberty?

One day, frustrated because he couldn't draw a chicken, my five-year-old father left the palace in haste. Grumbling his way through the forest, the rascal didn't pay attention to where he was going. He ended up in an unfamiliar meadow, with no clue whatsoever of where his home might be.

Finding himself lost and lonely, my father started shouting. He shouted so hard, that snakes abandoned their hides and birds ate their own feathers. He shouted so much that houses in Pleuron shook badly, the whole town had to be evacuated. He shouted so loud, that even the clouds were deafened. And yet my father kept shouting.

It was then when the centaur slapped my father. He slapped him hard on the cheek.

The centaur's name was Chiron, general of the army of the Northern kingdom of Ephyra. He was returning from a diplomatic mission in the nearby Calydon, when he bumped into my father.

Chiron hit my father so strongly, that the latter was thrown several meters away. My father stood up and looked at the centaur. He couldn't believe what had just happened. But the anger soon returned: with blind fury, he charged against the creature. My father was very strong, more than any man, but he was no match for an adult centaur: Chiron easily pinned him to the ground, and he kept him there until my father's tantrum was over.

Carrying my father on his back, Chiron brought him back to the palace. After a long discussion with my grandparents, it was decided that Chiron would take my father to Ephyra and give him an education.

And so my father left his homeland.

I guess that his mother didn't miss him much.

IV

    I wake up about an hour before the sun rises. The Priestess is sleeping peacefully. I walk some steps away from the bonfire and start my morning routine. First, I stretch my ankles, my legs and my back in different directions. Next, I strengthen my legs with three series of twenty one-legged squats. Then I do push-ups in a hand-stand, practice the bridge from standing position and back, do some ab exercises while I hang from a nearby tree. I finish with one-armed pullups hanging from a branch of the tree.
    The Priestess is clapping. I didn't notice her waking up.
    "Bravo, Thessalus! Are you training for the Olympic games?", she asks.
    "No. These are just some exercises that my father taught me."
    "Is that why you fight so well?"
    "I guess."
    "Well, training is over. Pack up your things, we're leaving."
    I think that she is acting bossy, but don't say anything. I roll my mat and pick up my broken sword and my bag. The Priestess takes some supplies from the carriage, folds them in her blanket and starts walking down the main road.
    We don't talk for a while. Everything is very quiet. A cool morning breeze blows over our faces while the sun rises. From time to time, we see small parcels of deer afar. As we walk the road, little squeaky noises give away hares and mice roaming on the sides. The Priestess looks pensive, perhaps she is thinking

about her late slaves. We have lunch at noon, under the shade of a willow.

In the afternoon, we hear a new sound: running water. The road leads to a turbulent river, crossed by a long wooden bridge. Two men discuss in the middle. One is tall like a tree, and well-built. He wears a straw hat and carries a club. The other one, clearly a merchant, tries to pass past the giant. Suddenly, the giant drops the club, grabs the merchant from the crotch and lifts him over his head. Then he throws his body down the bridge.

Before we can react, the waters have swallowed the merchant. I am frozen to the spot.

But the Priestess isn't. She crosses the bridge and faces the giant.

"What have you done?", she asks. "Why did you kill that man?"

The giant is smiling, but his eyes are cold. He has a round face, marked with smallpox.

"Welcome to Filippides' bridge. If you want to cross the bridge, you pay Filippides three dracmas. That gentleman over there", he says, pointing at the river, "wanted to cross the bridge for free. So I gently showed him the way out."

"Liar", replies the Priestess. "This bridge has no owner. When I crossed it one week ago, there was no murdering thug guarding it."

"You crossed my bridge!? Then it's six drachmas! Each!"

"I don't carry that much money, I'm afraid."

"Then get off my fucking bridge, you stingy aristocratic whore, before I make you eat a sandwich of your boyfriend's pussy!"

Without a word, the Priestess leaves the bridge. The giant seems very proud of himself. He keeps grinning, his hands on his waist.

The Priestess says:

"Don't worry, Thessalus, fighting that brute isn't worth it. There is another bridge a few kilometers up the river. That will just make our trip a couple of hours longer."

I still haven't laid foot on the bridge: all that time I was scared shitless of that ogre. I'm pondering the Priestess' plan when I notice the Harpy.

She is standing in front of the bridge, staring at me with her black eyes.

"Come on, let's go!", says the Priestess, pulling my arm. But I am not moving.

The Harpy's glance is stern. She doesn't need to say anything. I know what she thinks of me.

"Thessalus! Are you OK?"

"I need a moment", I say, dropping my blanket and my broken sword.

"Where are you going? No!", the Priestess implores.

While I walk towards the giant, I drop my bag, my bow and my quiver. I am full of rage.

The giant smiles, surprised.

"Oh, come on, Mr. Pussyflower, don't make me laugh...!"

I dash. He raises his arms to protect his body, but his body is not my target. I jump with both feet together and land on his left knee. I can hear it crack. Bouncing, I land on my hands and follow with a back handspring. I am standing again.

Screaming in pain, the giant falls on his knees. His hands go instinctively to the wounded knee. Now his head is within reach. It is now or never.

I approach him very fast and punch him on the nose with all my weight. I feel his nose bones splintering and his front teeth giving in. He falls like a trunk, surely dead.

My hands are trembling, I am so furious. I want to crush his skull, beat him until he has no head. Instead, I force myself to breathe deep. Once, twice, thrice.

When I get my shit together, I turn around and see that the Priestess is looking at me wide-eyed.

Avoiding her glance, I collect my things: my bow, my arrows, my bag, my mat and my sword.

"Please, come. The path is clear", I say.

The Priestess doesn't reply. She stares at me, accusing, for what feels like a minute.

Without a word, she grabs her blanket and crosses the bridge. She doesn't look back.

V

When the sun starts setting, we find a patch of barren land and camp there. Soon there is a bonfire, the Priestess' blanket is extended and we contemplate the fire where the salted meat roasts. We drink wine silently.

The Priestess has hardly said a word since the incident in the bridge. Neither have I, I feel too embarrassed. The Priestess looks pensive.

Finally, she speaks.

"I don't believe for a moment that you did that just to save a few hours on the way".

"He insulted you! He called you 'whore'!"

"You weren't trying to help me. If he had killed you, I would have had to continue the journey alone. You weren't thinking about me back then."

"But he murdered a man! You saw it!"

"Oh! So it wasn't about me, after all. You were trying to take justice into your own hands."

"Yes."

"That is not the reason why you attacked. First, we could have reported him at the nearest city. Second, if you just wanted him dead, you would have used your arrows."

"I wouldn't have had time. He was very close", I say, looking away.

The Priestess looks at me with severity. I raise my eyes, but can't hold her stare.

"Don't lie to me, young man, I've seen you shooting. He wouldn't have stood a chance. You wanted to kill that man with your hands. Why?"

"It's because of my father", I say.

"Your father. Did anything happen to him?"

"Someone-." I can feel the tears coming, I can't stop them. I can't keep talking, I can't breathe.

"Oh!"

Now she understands.

"A bandit?"

I nod. I start crying.

The Priestess comes next to me and hugs me. She puts my head on her lap and caresses my forehead. I think that I will never stop crying. That I have fallen into a hole, that I will never find my way up again.

I surprise myself telling her what happened last month. She doesn't look stern anymore. Instead, she listens with compassion.

When I finish, she asks me how I feel.

I tell her that I think about my father every day. That I always picture him coming from the fields, greeting me with his large hand. And smiling that big smile of his, the smile that made you want to die for him. The smile of the greatest man who ever lived. I miss him so much, my poor father, and I can't believe that he's not here anymore!

Some nights, I tell her, I dream of him. My father and I are at the farm, and he proposes to go for a walk. We chat and joke along the path to the forest. We eat dry beef near a small lake. We take a siesta under a big willow, side by side, listening to the song of the crickets. We act as if nothing had ever happened.

And then I wake up and it's dark and I'm alone, and I remember that my father is dead and I won't see him again.

I cry so much that, by the time I get a grip, the firewood is just embers.

The Priestess clears my tears with her scarf and throws some wood to the bonfire. I feel very tired and heavy, but I am not sleepy.

When the fire is high again, she speaks.

"Many years ago, a man came to my temple. The man had been a famous musician. He had played his lyre for kings and emperors. Artists from all over the world traveled to his home in Thracia to learn from him the art of music. He was loved and respected by all."

"And yet, when he arrived at Pallene, there were black circles under his eyes, his hair in shambles. His wife had died of a plague the previous summer, and he couldn't stop thinking about her. His music became so sad that he would leave audiences in tears. He stopped teaching. One day, though, he woke up with a plan. He had confessed the idea to a couple of friends and they had advised him to discuss the plan with me first."

"What plan?"

"The man intended to travel to mount Olympus to ask the Gods to return him his wife."

What? The world is spinning... Asking the gods to resurrect the dead...!

Meanwhile, the Priestess has continued:

"...plants, fungi, animals and humans die, but not immortals. Not only do they not age, but nothing in this world can bring their lives to an end. The musician was convinced that the al-mighty Olympian Gods could, if they wished, bring his wife back among the living."

"They certainly could. But, would they?"

"Well, that is the problem, isn't it? Gods do not care much about mortals' sorrows: they are too busy drinking nectar and fighting one another. The musician, however, thought that he could persuade them. He believed that, if he could just play his lyre for them for a moment, they would feel the pain in his heart and have compassion."

"So the man worked for a year on the piece that he would play for the Olympians. He composed his music inside a vaulted tomb: no one was allowed to listen to a single note. When he was done, he sold his land and his slaves, said goodbye to all his friends and started his pilgrimage to mount Olympus."

The Priestess concludes her story.

"The loss of the loving one is a stone tied to the neck. But it is a mistake to deal with it as if it were an external problem. With sorrow, there are no shortcuts. You will walk hundreds of miles looking for your father and you will see his mark everywhere you go. But you won't find him that way, Thessalus. Are you looking for your father? First find yourself. The moment you realize this, your quest will be over."

I stay silent for some minutes.

"What happened to the man in the story?", I ask. "Did he succeed?"

"What do you mean?"

"Did he talk to the gods?"

"I guess that he didn't", she replies, "because he never came back."

That night I have a dream. I am in a large wooden house, with many rooms. A hound howls outside. There are no windows, but I can feel that the sun is set.

In the rooms, I hear people talking and walking around, but I can see nobody. A woman speaks about her little daughter, she wonders who will give her shelter. An old man talks over and over about a sea battle in Ionia. A young lover asks where his loved one is. I talk them back, but they don't hear.

A heart is beating. I follow the sound up some stairs and end up facing a large wooden door. I cross the threshold and find my father.

He is lying on a large bed. He is very skinny, a sack of bones. Blood is flowing from a large wound on his chest. He looks asleep. When I get close, though, he opens his eyes widely and stares at me.

"I don't know how much I can withstand", he says.

Around his bed there are trays with food: goat, boar, cheese. Everything looks delicious! But it's made of ashes.

Suddenly, my father looks confused.

"Thessalus, where is your mother? What is this? What am I doing here?"

He tries to stand up, but he's too weak to even sit on the bed.

"I want to go home, Thessalus! I want to go home! I want to go home!"

Holding his arms, I cry: "Father!"

I wake up. I am curled in my mat, in front of an extinguished bonfire. The Priestess sleeps deeply next to me. I am trembling, my eyes full of tears.

I make up my mind then.

VI

The centaur Chiron raised my father as his own son. He taught him to read poetry, play the lyre and fight. My father mastered one out of three.

From the very beginning, it was clear to Chiron that my father had a talent for war. Not only was he impossibly strong, but also very fast and agile. In addition, he showed great coordination: already at the age of ten, he was able to fend himself from two skilled swordsmen attacking simultaneously.

Thus Chiron taught my father how to master the sword, the bow, the spear and the shield. Under his thorough supervision, my father also learned to control his strength. Chiron would make him stand and do push-ups on one hand while caressing a little mouse with the other. He would make my father fight a bear with a raw egg in each fist. He would bury him in sand completely and make him stay like that for hours, breathing through a bamboo cane.

There was one problem, though. In armed combat, my father could never unleash all his power: his best blows made spears splinter and daggers melt. Swords would break in his hand like loafs of bread.

"The problem is not you", said Chiron, "it's your weapons. The sword of a warrior must be stronger than the warrior himself; that stands to reason. What you need is a sword that can resist even your hardest thrusts".

Only one blacksmith could forge that sword: the crippled god Hephaestus. From his large furnace in mount Olympus, the son of Zeus and Hera had been crafting for eons the tools and weapons of the gods.

The artisan who built Apollo's golden chariot could surely make a sword that my father couldn't break.

Hence Chiron and my father traveled to Olympus to request an audience with him.

When they arrived at Hephaestus' palace, they found two people discussing at the gates. One was a short hairy man with a very deep voice. He had muscled arms and a large torso, but his legs were short and weak like a child's. The man was talking to a 30-year old woman. She wore a white dress and had a very elegant face, her glare full of intelligence. Chiron greeted them with a smile. Then he introduced my father to Hephaestus and Athena.

Very agitated, Hephaestus explained Chiron that he had lost control of one of his mechanical automata. The animated statue was walking around Hephaestus' workshop, shooting steel arrows to whomever approached. This had happened weeks ago, and ever since not even the bravest cyclops would dare enter the palace's cellar.

My father offered Hephaestus to subdue the broken machine. Hephaestus promised him that, should he be successful, he would forge for him the best sword ever made.

Chiron, Athena and Hephaestus accompanied my father to the stairs which led to the cellar. Since my father didn't carry any weapons with him, Hephaestus lent him his hammer. And down he went.

At the end of the stairs, my father found a small metal door ajar. Peeking in, he saw the killing machine working with hammer and tongs on the anvil. A large metallic structure next to the Automaton lied on the workshop bench.

The Automaton was four meters tall, and entirely made of iron. Its circular head had very large ears and a permanently open wide mouth. Its four arms were wide like tree trunks and ended in hands the size of a dog. From each finger sprouted a handful of blades, that the machine used from time to time to manipulate the metallic structure on the bench.

As soon as my father set foot on the room, the machine dropped the hammer and the tongs and turned around. Then it started walking towards my father.

The Automaton was approaching my father with an unnaturally constant speed, sorting ingots and metal carcasses on the workshop floor, as if nothing could delay its course, all the while emitting a very loud sound, like a howl. Its sixty 50 cm-long blades were all spread, pointing at my father's head. The Automaton was going to kill my father!

Or so it would have, had it not been a hundred meters away from him. As soon as my father realized what was going on, he threw his hammer at the Automaton's head, that exploded in a thousand pieces. The Automaton collapsed on the floor, therefrom it would not raise again.

"That was fairly easy!", said my father, while he picked up his hammer, a big smile on his face.

Curious to see what it was that the Automaton had been working on, my father approached the working bench.

There he found an almost exact replica of the machine he had just destroyed. My father was pondering why an Automaton would make a statue of itself, when the replica moved.

Surprised, my father stepped back, just to see the replica stand on its legs! The replica only had three arms, but otherwise looked just as mortal as its dead creator. Without further delay, my father kicked the legs of the new Automaton, that loudly fell on the ground. Then he used Hephaestus' hammer to crush its head.

Some movement in his periphery made my father aware that he was not alone. Two more automata had entered the workshop through a door beyond the forge, possibly leading to a storage room. A third automaton was just crossing the threshold. The three machines were walking towards my father, as determined as their creator, and howling in the same horrific way. When they started shooting arrows, my father dashed out of the place.

Once outside the cellar, my father grabbed one of the columns of Hephaestus' palace and used it to block the entrance, just as dozens of automata were climbing up the stairs. Then he recounted Chiron, Hephaestus and Athena what he had seen.

Chiron and the gods had a short deliberation. On one hand, there was enough material in the workshop to build a whole army of automata, something that the original Automaton might have already done: removing the column and fighting them all was out of the question. On the other hand, the column would keep the automata in the cellar for a while, but not indefinitely. They had to find a solution quickly, before the machines took over Olympus!

Finally, Athena said:

"I have a plan, but it will require large amounts of sand. Thasus, take this", she said, handing my father a small sack.

"I want you to travel East", she added. "At some point you will see a large beach. Please collect as much sand as you can and bring it here."

My father looked at the sack with scorn.

"Do you think that such a ridiculous amount of sand is going to make any difference? Why don't you give me a bigger sack?"

"Oh, that sack's all right", Athena replied. "I weaved it myself."

Obedient, my father walked East for a day and a night. When the next day dawned, he found himself in a beautiful beach, full of the finest white sand.

My father then started to fill Athena's sack. However, something strange happened: no matter how much sand my father threw in the sack, the latter didn't seem to fill. After a few hours, there was a large crater on the beach, and Athena's sack felt so heavy that my father couldn't hold it in one hand. Thus he returned to Olympus. Shortly after he departed, the tide rose, and the waters of the Aegean sea flooded the sand crater, forming the Gulf of Salonika.

Upon his return, the gods were marveled to see the amount of sand that my father had managed to gather; most of all, Athena, who could no longer carry the sack herself.

It was time to put Athena's plan in motion. At her signal, Chiron and Hephaestus removed the column blocking the entrance to the workshop. Immediately, my father opened Athena's sack and filled the cellar with sand.

Metallic noises, knocks and grunts followed. Something was moving under the sand!

After some minutes, an Automaton's arm emerged. My father stood in front of Athena, ready to die protecting the goddess. The Automaton crossed the threshold, facing them, its rotating blades ready to dismember gods, humans and centaurs alike.

And all of a sudden, the blades ceased moving. The sand was blocking the gears of the machine, which could not rotate its blades any longer in either direction. Soon the sand blocked the legs as well, and the Automaton fell on the palace's marble floor with a loud clank.

In the next few hours, several other automata managed to reach the cellar gate, most of them already half-paralyzed. They would walk a few meters more and then lose balance. With great enthusiasm, Thasus and Hephaestus hammered each fallen automaton until it did not have a single cog left. The rebellion of the machines had failed.

Grateful, Hephaestus honored his promise to my father: as soon as they removed all the sand from the workshop, he and his cyclops forged an excellent double-edged steel sword, that my father called Diana. In addition, Hephaestus crafted for him a corselet and a winged helmet. The sword, the armor and the winged helmet: that is how my father always appears in reliefs, drawings and statuettes.

A hero had been born.

VII

I examine my father's sword in the light of the morning. I was wishing for Hephaestus to secretly come and repair it during the night. But, no: Diana is still broken.

The Priestess finally wakes up. Today she has missed the show; I already did my exercises. In fact, we have both overslept; it is almost midday.

The Priestess is smiling at the sun. She seems so content! I wish I could share her peace. She greets me with her hand.

"Good morning, Thessalus! Did you sleep well?"

"Not so well, madam. I had a lot to think about."

She stares at me for some seconds.

"You're going to do it."

Seriously, how can she read me so easily?

"I think so, yes."

"My bad". She looks down. "I shouldn't have put those silly ideas in your head." She adds: "I guess I can't change your mind, can I?"

I shake my head.

She stands up. "All right, then let's get going. If we hurry, we might arrive at my temple in time for lunch."

We collect out belongings and return to the road.

Along the way, the Priestess talks a lot. She speaks of long-lost treasures and ancient sea battles. She recites poetry in the old language and talks about peoples of faraway lands.

#

My mind must have wandered, because now the Priestess is giving me all kinds of advice for my journey. In fact, she tells me everything that will happen to me: she explains where I will go, whom I will meet, the mistakes I will make, the challenges I will face.

But something weird happens: I cannot keep in mind anything she says! As soon as she reaches the end of a sentence, I have forgotten the beginning.

Just one thing sticks: at the very end, I meet my father.

I find him in a palace. My father and I stare at each other, and then my quest is over.

#

Before I realize it, the Priestess and I are in front of a very large temple, with four columns in the facade. This must be Pallene. The sun is very high; I must have lost the sense of time. Two slaves come out of the temple and take the Priestess' bag.

The Priestess turns to me.

"What will you do next?", she asks. "Do you want to stay for the night?"

"No, thanks", I answer. "I'd rather start my journey right away."

"I understand."

She looks at me for some seconds. She smiles.

"Thessalus, I wish to thank you for accompanying me back to my temple. I don't own many things, but I want to give you something."

She opens her tunic, revealing a pendant hanging from her neck. It is a black leather strip, with a holed coin tied to the middle. She unties the pendant and ties it to my neck.

I look at the coin. It is aging-green. On one side, there is the image of a woman wearing a helmet: she holds a spear on one hand; a bird on the other one. I can't read the other side of the coin, the picture is worn-out.

"No one accepts them anymore, but they make very good necklaces", she says.

I let the coin drop inside my tunic. The coin feels warm against my skin.

Suddenly, the Priestess hugs me.

"Goodbye, Thessalus!", she whispers.
Nodding, I pick up my stuff and leave.

VIII

My next destination is Athens. I don't know the exact way to mount Olympus; Athens is the perfect place to procure myself a map. Besides, I need to get Diana repaired.

I reach the city in about three hours. The road is paved, with graves and family plots on each side. One of them catches my glance: it is the tomb of a man. It has a relief, where he is sitting on a chair, holding hands with a standing young man, perhaps his son. Their faces show no grief, they are inexpressive, as if death were not a big matter after all.

Every year, in spring, my father took me to Athens. In the morning, we would sell sheep skins in the Agora. By midday, we would browse the market stands, looking at statuettes and mechanical inventions. We would eat dry meat at the Zeus Stoa, where my father would discuss long and loud with sophists and other unemployed. In the afternoon, we would watch the theater contest: nine tragedies and three satyr plays. It was so exciting! When the chorus announced the end of the show, my father and I would walk to an inn near the Potter's quartier. I would sleep like a trunk.

While I walk my way through the city, I remember following my father's shadow through those very same streets, many-many years ago. It was a sunny midday. I must have been quite young, for I had problems to keep up with my father's pace. And there was also the smell... Athens' houses looked to me small and crammed, they had garbage buckets in front of every household. The whole city stank.

Close to the Dipylon gate, I find a blacksmith. I pay him two drachmas and he promises to have my sword ready by next morning. That means that I must spend the night in Athens. I consider the idea of sleeping outside, in the fields, but decide against it: there are too many people around to worry about. I'd rather find an inn. Money is not an issue: bandits have it in abundance.

Next, I go to the Agora. There are so many stands! Selling groceries, papyri, wooden toys, colored minerals from the far east… After a while, I locate the stand of a cartographer. He is bald and wrinkled, and very friendly. I explain him that I am traveling to mount Olympus.

He looks puzzled.

"What for? There is nothing there! Are you sure you don't want a map of Rhodes? I hear that this is the place to be for a young and ambitious chap."

"No, thanks. I need to travel to mount Olympus."

"Mount Olympus comprises a very large area. Which part do you want to visit exactly?"

"Mount Mytikas."

He is startled.

"The home of the gods?"

"Yes."

He stares at me. He doesn't understand.

"Why are you traveling to Olympus?", he asks.

"That is my business", I answer.

"OK, then. Let me draw you a map."

He places a blank papyrus on the table. Then he writes the four cardinal signs.

"Look, young man…" He draws a convex shape on the bottom of the papyrus. "This is Athens. We are here." He writes 'Athens' in the middle of the shape. Next, he marks the upper part of the shape with a cross. "And this is the Acharnian gate. You must leave the city here."

He adds more and more marks, with names like Thespia, Hyria, Livadeia… He also draws some natural accidents to guide me through my journey: a river, a lake, a small mountain... He concludes with a triangle at the top of the papyrus.

"... and this is Peak Mytikas", he says. "Up there it is very cold, I advise you to wear a very thick tunic. Sometimes, there is even snow!"

"What is snow?"

"It is something white, and so cold that it burns your fingers. It is made of water, you see?"

I don't believe him, but nod anyway.

He hands me the papyrus, that I stick in my bag. Next I offer him some obols, but he refuses to take them.

"It's OK, boy. This is on the house."

He is looking at me with a very worried expression. It's making me feel very uncomfortable, so I don't discuss with him: I say 'thank you' and leave.

Sometimes atheists look at me that way, as if I were nuts. I hate it. I am not nuts, I am just not an atheist. Just because more and more people think that there are no gods, that doesn't make them right. It doesn't mean that everyone agrees with them either. He surely thinks that I won't find anything in Mytikas, that I'll return empty-handed. Well, we'll see.

Angry, I wander aimlessly around the Agora. I stop at a very strange stand. It consists exclusively of clockworks. I had seen them as a kid, when a merchant passed by our village. A wooden bird flapping its wings. A carriage with a horse that rolls by itself.

But this stand... There is a metal theater the size of a bucket. On the stage, I see a white surface with a black drawing of a bearded man fighting a large snake. What is out of the ordinary is that both drawings, the man's and the snake's, are moving! The snake coils around the man, who, after a brief struggle, manages to free himself. Then the surface turns white again, and the same man is leading an army towards another one. Swords clash for a while, and then a figure from the other army emerges. The man and the figure fight, but then all the characters merge to form a spinning spiral. Finally, the surface turns white again.

I can't believe my eyes. Have I gone mad?

The merchant intervenes. "Not bad, ha? This beauty comes from Rhodes."

"What were those little beings? Are they nymphs?"

He laughs. "Oh, no! They're just pictures I drew in a long papyrus. They appear quickly one after the other, so it looks as if they moved."

I don't understand him completely, but I get the general idea.

"Please have a look at this wonder!", he says, while calling attention to a large vase on the other side of the stand.

The vase is made of bronze, with two handles. It has a slot on top and a spout on the side.

The merchant hands me a clay glass. "Put it under the spout", he says. I do as I'm told. "Now, place a drachma in the slot."

I look at him.

"Trust me! Put a drachma in the slot, if you want the blessing of the gods."

I drop a coin in the slot. There is a "clink" sound and then water flows from the spout to the glass until the latter fills. Then I hear another "clink", and the water ceases to flow.

"This water is blessed by Ares", he says, "it will bring you luck."

I have lost a drachma, but what a show!

"In that case", I say, "cheers to Ares!", and bring the glass to my lips.

Then something hits me hard up on the skull and I close my eyes for a moment.

IX

When I open my eyes, I am lying on the floor. My mouth kisses the ground and my hands are tied behind my back. My legs are also tied. Two voices, one deep and another one high-pitched are having a very lively discussion.

"There is a procedure, you know", says the high-pitched voice. "We can't just kill a bandit on the spot."

"Fuck off! I'm not asking you to kill him! I'm asking you to let ME kill him!", replies the deep voice.

That voice... With a headache, I arch my back and look up. I can't believe my eyes.

"The giant!", I mumble. His left leg is bandaged and bent: he stands on a crutch. His mouth and nose are black: I'm surprised that he's still alive!

"Ah, he is awake!", says the high-pitched voice. It belongs to a law-enforcement slave. He is short, but muscled. He carries a baton on his waist.

He turns me around. Then I see that he and the giant are not alone: there are some other officers around, as well as some bystanders.

"This monster!", the giant says, pointing at me with his large index, "this terrible, terrible bandit! He viciously assaulted me while I was peacefully ambling my way through our beautiful Greek landscape. He broke my leg and my teeth and left me for dead! Who knows how many people this dangerous villain might have murdered in cold blood? I was lucky enough to recognize him in the Agora and call the law enforcement patrol. And now we're supposed to have considerations with this beast? My Athenian brothers and sisters, I say: to the cliff with him!"

The crowd cheers. So do some of the officers.

"Citizens, that is not the way we do things here!", says a man. He is thin and tall, has very black hair and wears a blue tunic. He is very handsome. "I am Orestes, magistrate of Athens, and I hereby claim this case. I will make sure that all the proper judicial steps are followed by the book. To begin, this despicable criminal deserves to have an impartial trial…" He looks at the sun dial. "… at five. Are there any volunteers to sentence this man to death?"

A large tumult erupts. It seems that everyone in the Agora wants to be my jury! While the magistrate annotates names in a papyrus, the slave with the high-pitched voice and another officer lift me up and bring me to one of the surrounding buildings.

It is, of course, the prison. After noting down my name, the guards bring me to the cellar and lock me in a cell. Only then one of the guards cuts my ties. I don't know why, but they let me keep the map.

"You might better prepare your defense", says the guard. "The citizens are rabid: they haven't had an execution for years!" He leaves.

I look around the cell. It is square and small, one can just walk ten steps from side to side. A couple of rickety hay mattresses lie on the floor. Along the walls there are some benches, where four people sit staring at me.

Three of them are old hags. They have long grey hair and wear filthy dresses. They whisper at each other and laugh among themselves. The fourth person is smiling at me. He is fat and old, and mostly bald. His glance is jumping from me to the women, as if he were trying to watch us simultaneously. I can feel a torrent of manic energy bubbling up behind those old restless eyes.

All of a sudden, he walks towards me. He speaks fast and fluent, as if he were reciting a poem.

"Young man! Welcome to our modest cell!" He shakes my hand. "My name is Mr. Vertigo."

The women laugh.

"Why are they laughing?", I ask.

"Ha, ha! Because my name is *not* Mr. Vertigo!"

Before I can process this, he points at the three old women and adds: "please let me introduce you to my enchanting associates." The women giggle, pleased.

"Is this your first time in prison?", he asks.

"Yes."

"What happened?"

"I beat up a man."

"Your sincerity touches me."

"But wait! He was evil!"

"Of course he was!"

"No, seriously, he was as evil as it gets. I saw him throwing a man over a bridge!"

"Aha! So he's a murderer. He killed a man and then you punished him."

"I guess I did."

"Say no more, my boy! To my eyes, this case is crystal-clear. No sane jury would punish an honest young citizen who fights for justice with his fists."

"Hell, no!", says one of the women.

"It would be the end of civilization!", shouts another one.

"Guards! Release this boy! He's innocent as a lamb!", says the third one.

"What is your name, young man?", asks Mr. Vertigo.

"I am Thessalus, son of Thasus."

"On top, you are the son of one of our national heroes!?", he cries. "Then believe me when I say that you will walk out a free man. Fear not your upcoming trial, young Thessalus. The gods are with you!"

"Should I prepare something for the court? A speech, or some sort of statement …?"

"Certainly not! A scripted discourse will make you sound artificial and dishonest. Don't address the jury, Thessalus: talk to them. If you explain these people who you are and what you did, and you speak from the heart, the jury will not fail to see the purity of your intentions."

Mr. Vertigo is full of charisma. However, I am not fully convinced.

"If telling the truth is enough to get one out of jail, what are you four doing here?", I ask.

"Very simple, my boy", he replies. "Telling the truth only helps when you haven't committed a crime."

"What did you do?", I ask.

He gestures towards the three women and himself. "We were accused of corrupting the youth."

The four of them burst out laughing.

X

Sometime later, the officer returns. Through the bars of the cell, he chains my hands behind my back. Only then he opens the cell's door.

He takes me back to the Agora. Surrounded by a choir of shouting strangers, we walk towards another building on the border of the square. The guard was right: these people are rabid. Some threaten me; others insult me; others spit at me. Most of them just laugh. The crowd keeps following us to the entrance of the building, where a few slaves are having a hard time keeping them out.

The guard says: "those are the ones who were not selected to be part of the jury."

"Lucky me!", I reply.

"The jury is much more emotional, you'll see."

We enter the court. It is a very large room, with a small table in the middle, where magistrate Orestes awaits. Beside him there is a scribe sitting on a stool, a large blank papyrus on his lap. In front of the table there are two separate benches. The giant sits on the farthest one, on the right. While the guard takes me to the other bench, I see that there are many seating rows around the room. There must be a thousand people sitting on those rows. Everyone is silent.

When I take my seat, magistrate Orestes starts talking.

"Members of the jury! You are summoned today to arbitrate in a certainly unusual case. This trial has not been announced by writing notice. This obeys to the particular nature of the crime that we will investigate today."

Still staring at the jury, he points at me.

"The accused is said to be a bandit, an outcast, an outlaw. Not residing in Athens, we cannot trust that he would attend his own trial. Hence the judiciary has had to settle this sudden procedure."

He turns to me.

"Young man, what is your name?"

"Thessalus, son of Thasus."

The jury gets mad: everybody is shouting! A man's voice sticks out. He is fat and wears a black tunic. "You have no shame! Death to the heretic!", he cries. The giant is laughing.

"Order!", shouts the magistrate. "Young man, that is not funny. You are in the house of law, and you're required to show due respect. What is your *real* name?".

"I am Thessalus, son of Thasus!"

This time the magistrate cannot contain the uproar. A man abandons the rows and starts advancing towards my bench. The officer quickly draws his sword and stands between him and me. The man returns to his seat.

The guard whispers: "son! The figure of Thasus is very dear to us Athenians. You're putting the whole jury against you!"

When the jury is silent, the magistrate addresses me again.

"Once again, boy: who are you?"

"Thessalus."

"That's better. Please note that down", he tells the scribe.

He points at the giant.

"Accuser, please stand up and say your name."

The giant stands up. He looks like a monster.

"I am Sweet Filippides."

"Scribe, note his name down."

"I protest!", I shout. "'Sweet'!? You are a monster! I saw you throwing a man down a bridge! Who would call you 'sweet'?"

He looks at me very stern.

"My late grandmother!"

The jury moans: "ohhhh...!" Then they start booing me. I cannot help but feel that my trial is not going in the right direction.

The magistrate intervenes. "Silence everyone! And you", he says, pointing at me, "shall only talk when I give you permission."

"Shut your mouth, you disrespectful motherfucker!", says the giant.

"Well said, Sweet Filippides", says the magistrate. "Now, please, present your allegations."

Filippides stands up and looks at the crowd.

"Good people of Athens! Yesterday afternoon, I went to the countryside for a walk. I was merrily collecting wildflowers for my sick aunt, when this criminal, this murderer, appeared out of nowhere and hit me on the knee with a wooden sledge hammer."

"Even while I was falling on the floor, I could not but feel compassion for that lost soul. 'Young man, calm down!', I implored him. 'Let us dialog like reasonable human beings'. But this contemptible beast, this dangerous monster, just smiled like a crocodile and spat: 'oh, but I *love* beating Athenians! Their soft flesh is to my fists like clay to the sculptor. I will keep robbing, murdering and kidnapping Athenians. And no one, not even an Athenian court of justice, will ever stop me from spreading evil wherever I go. Hahahaha!'. Then he smashed my face with his hammer and I passed out."

"Who knows what kind of desecrations this wild animal did to my unconscious body? By the time I woke up, the sun was setting. Lucky me, a goodhearted fellow merchant offered to take me to Athens in his carriage. As soon as I arrived at the city, I limped to a nearby fountain to wash my face. Why? Because I still intended to visit my sick sister later, that is how good a brother I am! Then, reflected in the water, I saw *this*."

He points to his face.

"Look at me, my fellow Athenians! Until yesterday, I was a very handsome man. I was the heir of Eros, the envy of Adonis! Young women got wet at my mere sight. The queen of Thebes promised to eat her husband and children alive if I agreed to marry her! I have laid with a different muscled boy every night for the last ten years. And now...", he points to his face again, "...*this*."

"Contemplate this horrible mask! The broken teeth, the underdeveloped jaw, the beardless cheeks. This is not a human face, it is the face of the Gorgon! Not even my sick brother-in-law can stand the sight of me! Now I am doomed to spend the rest of my days alone: without a shoulder to rest, hugging myself till I fall sleep during the long winter nights."

He points at me.

"I curse you, you miserable bandit! You have stolen my life!"

The members of the jury cry disconsolately. The man with the black tunic shouts: "scum! Bandit! Death to the shameless scoundrel!"

"Silence!", the magistrate demands. He turns to me. "Young Thessalus, did you inflict this pious man those horrible wounds?"

I stutter. "Yes, but-but-but…"

"He admits it!", interrupts Sweet Filippides.

"He has no shame!", shouts the man in black. "He's beyond redemption! Death to the stranger!"

"Jeez!", the guard mumbles, "I had never seen the grave digger so agitated!"

"Let me finish!", I shout.

The jury replies: "oooooh!"

"Yesterday this man was extorting money from people who wanted to cross a bridge. A merchant refused to pay, and he threw him to the water! That's why I attacked him!"

But the jury is skeptical.

"What!?", I say. "He's a menace! Someone had to do something!"

"Shut up! You're making a fool of yourself!", says the giant. "One minute ago you were claiming to be great Thasus…"

"I am Thessalus! Thasus was my fa…"

"…and now you dare accusing the accuser! Well, let me tell you something, young man. Our legal system, the best in the world, is based on the scientific principle that the first to complain is always to be believed. And who are you to question a scientific principle? Are you a natural philosopher, by chance?"

"I…"

"That's what I thought. The jury shall now vote."

The magistrate exclaims: "that is for me to say!"

The magistrate stares at the jury for a few seconds.

"The jury shall now vote", he concludes.

The members of the jury leave their seats and queue in front of a small door at the back of the room.

Filippides says to the magistrate: "Sir, you delivered the line much better than me. How confident you looked! And the pause at the beginning...!"

"Thank you, Sweet Filippides. I have a lot of practice, you know."

I ask the guard: "now what happens?"

He sighs. "Each member of the jury has two discs: one with Filippides' name on it; the other one, with yours. They will deposit one of them in an urn in that room". He points at the back door. "At the end, the discs are counted: the one with more discs wins the suit."

I look at the queue. Some members of the jury are making signs of decapitation.

After the jury returns the rows, we wait for some more minutes. Then, a slave approaches the magistrate and gives him a piece of papyrus.

The magistrate stands.

"Everyone stand up!"

We obey.

"These are the results of the vote. Members in favor of the accuser Sweet Filippides: 1001. Members in favor of, er, the boy: none. I don't think we need a recount."

The jury laughs. The giant laughs *very* hard.

"Next, each part will propose a sentence. Young man, tell us: what do you think you deserve?"

My legs tremble, my heart beats loudly. I must go for corporal punishment: this crowd will take nothing less. Perhaps ten lashes?

When I look up to answer Orestes, I find the Harpy perching on the magistrate's desk.

She feels my fear, my lack of manliness. She can feel my shame.

Coward.

"Go fuck yourselves", I say to the jury. "This man is a murderer and you are a bunch of morons. I hope that he assaults you the very next time you travel alone. That way, your last thought before dying will be: 'I'm an imbecile!'"

The jury gasps.

The magistrate says: "young man! You must propose a fair sentence!"

"You want a fair sentence? Let me crack this bastard's head open. That's fair". The last two sentences sound like grunts. I am so angry that I can't speak properly.

The giant stands up.

"Dear citizens! This cold-blooded criminal is a threat to our society. His acts and his words show a complete lack of remorse, he is obviously beyond redemption. What do you do with a wild lion? You give it mercy! For the life of my sick cousin, I ask you to sentence this delinquent to death by falling!"

The jury roars.

My arms are tied, but my legs are free. Before the guard can do something about it, I stand up, and, running towards the giant, I execute a somersault, landing on his good knee. I hear a "crack!", and feel it bending the other way. The giant falls to the floor, shouting in agony.

The jury is shouting in disbelief.

I have no time to waste. Lading on the giant's back, I scissor his neck with my legs. We roll on the floor. He is trying to pry my legs open, but I am stronger than him. It is just a matter of time…

… but, alas!, I am too slow. Before I can crack the giant's neck, the guard beats my head with the hilt of his sword.

And everything turns dark again…

XI

I wake up in the cell. The little window shows a dark sky. It's night. My head rests on the lap of one of the old women, she is caressing my hair. It should be hurting like hell, but, strangely, I feel all right. I sit down.

Mr. Vertigo approaches the bench and grabs my shoulder.

"Thessalus! How are you? The guard told us how you broke your accuser's leg. He said that it was very impressive!"

I'm still confused. "The guard... he beat me... on the head..."

"He was doing his job, no hard feelings."

"What happened next?"

"You got sentenced to death by falling."

"Ah, yes. Damn...!". All of a sudden, my head hurts so much that I don't care.

But something doesn't fit. "If I got sentenced, what am I doing here? Why didn't they execute me while I was unconscious?"

"Tonight begins the wine festival of Anthesteria", says Mr. Vertigo. "No executions are allowed until the end of the festivities, in two days' time."

"Our executions were also delayed", says one of the old women.

"How inconvenient!", says another one.

"What a shame!", says the third.

"But don't worry, Thessalus", says Mr. Vertigo. "We'll find something to do in the meantime."

Mr. Vertigo keeps talking and talking, but I can't follow the conversation. In fact, I have problems to keep my eyes open.

Mr. Vertigo looks at me weirdly. "You look very tired, young Thessalus", he says. "I think it's time for you to rest."

Suddenly, I hear a loud, high-pitched whistle, like the note of a flute. It is very bothering, it drives me nuts!

Then I must have fallen asleep, because I can't remember what happened next.

XII

When he turned 20, my father decided that it was time to return to Pleuron. He wished to make amendments with his parents and claim his succession rights to the royal throne. Thus he packed his winged helmet, his armor and his sword, said goodbye to Chiron and left Ephyra for good.

When my father turned up at the court of Pleuron, though, my grandfather Antiochus was not overwhelmed with joy: he still remembered the little brat who used to terrorize the kingdom. Consequently, Antiochus made his soldiers arrest my father and confined him in the darkest and tiniest cell of the palace's dungeons.

My father could have broken his chains and escaped from the prison at any time. However, out of respect for my grandfather, he remained in his little cell.

For one year, Antiochus refused to visit his son in prison, not even once. The night of the anniversary of my father's incarceration, Antiochus had a dream.

He was on the summit of a tall mountain. It was cold and windy. In front of him stood a big marble palace. To protect himself from the wind, my grandfather entered it.

Inside, there was an open space, surrounded by columns. In the center, an olive tree stood on a platform. An owl rested on one of its branches.

Antiochus guessed that he was in mount Olympus, in the temple of the goddess Athena. Soon, a woman of around thirty left the main building and walked towards my grandfather. She was pale, and had a very elegant face. Very confidently, she stood before my grandfather and said:

"Antiochus! What are you doing to your son?"

"My son is very dangerous, your Highness, a wild man!", replied Antiochus. "If I let him free, who knows what kind of havoc he will cause?"

The woman looked at him sternly.

"Your son has traveled from Ephyra to implore your pardon. He has spent a year in prison just to win your heart. Give him a chance to redeem, Antiochus. Your kingdom will thank you."

When Antiochus woke up, he visited his son's cell. He found my father in a terrible state: he was pale as plaster, he smelled strongly of sweat and his face was hidden behind a very thick beard.

Antiochus explained my father that neither he nor his subjects had forgiven my father's behavior. However, he offered my father a way to regain their confidence. For a whole year, Antiochus would entrust my father with a number of labors. If my father refused or was unable to carry any of them, he would have to abandon Pleuron forever.

My father accepted the deal.

And so the story of my father's three labors starts.

XIII

I am awakened by the sound of the crotalum, the rhoptron and the salpinx. For a moment, the high volume makes me think that all those instruments must be inside my head. I open my eyes and look through the cell window.

What I see is a sea of sandals: running, dancing and marching. There is a big racket outside: all the city seems to be chanting and laughing.

"Good morning, Thessalus!", says Mr. Vertigo. "How did you sleep?".

"Not bad", I answer. It is true: I feel strong like a bull.

He and the three women look at me with expectation.

"What?", I ask.

Mr. Vertigo comes close and says: "it is time to explain you our little plan!".

"Your plan?", I shout. The noise from the street is unbearable.

He raises his index to his lips. "Please, Thessalus, discretion!", he whispers in my ear.

He points to the right of the cell door. "This wall", he whispers, "connects this cell with an empty open cell. The wall is made of plaster. A strong young man like you could tear it down in half and hour!"

I stand up and examine the cell wall. It is made of plaster indeed, but I would break my knuckles open if I tried to demolish it with my bare fists.

"No way", I conclude.

"Ino, show him", says Mr. Vertigo.

One of the old women, sitting on the bench, opens her legs and a metal ball the size of a melon rolls down and crashes on the floor.

"Ino had been holding that ball for three days, ever since the four of us were apprehended. Good job, Ino!"

The woman giggles.

"Go on, boy! Take the ball and tear down the wall."

"But they'll hear us!"

"No, they won't. Because, from this moment on, this cell is also celebrating Anthesteria!". He turns to the women: "Girls! One, two, three!"

Mr. Vertigo and the three women start singing along with the people outside. The women clap their hands loudly, while Mr. Vertigo bangs his hands on the bench. They are making quite a stir!

A guard upstairs shouts: "shut up!"

Mr. Vertigo shouts back: "or what? You'll put us in prison?". The women laugh and keep clapping.

Mr. Vertigo signals me to start: it's demolition time! I pick up the ball and start hitting the wall.

Very soon, there is a wide tunnel connecting the two cells. Singing all along, each of us passes through the hole to the adjacent chamber. As Mr. Vertigo promised, the door is unlocked.

We sing and sing, while we go up the stairs. Mr. Vertigo and the old women dance and clap while I knock unconscious the two guards in the reception. We dance our way out of the prison.

Outside, the Agora has turned into a crowded party. There are people everywhere, singing and stamping their feet, making noise with their crotala. Somebody hands me a bowl of wine and a yellow clay theater mask depicting sadness. I tie it around my head on and turn to see my new friends wearing new costumes. The women have white masks of happiness, and Mr. Vertigo wears the mask of a bearded man with a crazy expression. He has somehow gotten hold of a staff of giant fennel.

We drink, sing and piss our way out of the Agora. We get into fights, we hug strangers, we kiss dogs and cats. We lift Mr. Vertigo over our heads, as if in a procession. When we reach the Potter's quartiers, I bump into the blacksmith: for a bottle of wine, he agrees to open his workshop and hand me Diana. My sword looks so immaculate! I try to make some feints, but I'm too drunk and fall on the floor. Mr. Vertigo laughs. The women laugh. I laugh.

We are still laughing when we leave Athens through the Acharnian gate. Mr. Vertigo and the women have acquired an absurd amount of wine amphoras. Sometimes we run, euphoric.

When we can't walk or drink anymore, when the sun is setting behind the Northern hills, when the crickets sing and the owl hoots, we five settle along the path. By then I can hardly see straight. The women make a bonfire in some manner, and we all crowd around it. Suddenly, one of the old women stands up, sniffing.

"I come back soon", she says, and dashes through the fields. Man, she is fast.

She returns a short time later, with a dead hare in her hands. Her mouth is covered in blood.

"Thanks, Autonoe", says Mr. Vertigo.

The woman drops the hare on the lap of another woman and lies down a bit further from our circle. The other woman starts skinning the hare, and very soon we are all eating a roast.

"Come here, Thessalus", says Mr. Vertigo. "I want to show you something."

Staggering, I get close and drop by his side.

"Look!", he says. He holds a miserable obol in his right hand.

He shakes it very fast, and it turns into a drachma!

Next he tries to break the drachma, and the latter turns into two drachmas, that he breaks into four, that he breaks into eight drachmas!

He tries to break them again, but this time the drachmas explode in a cascade of obols.

I look into his eyes, incredulous. "How…?".

"How what?", he replies.

I glance down. Both of his hands are empty.

I am speechless! My father knew a couple of tricks with coins, but I had never seen such mastery, not even among the itinerant musicians.

"Did you like it?", he says.

"It was amazing", I say. "You're an extraordinary performer!"

"A performer… yes, I guess that's what I am now", he says, disappointed. Suddenly he looks very old and tired. "Long time ago, I used to do real magic. I would make lions and bears appear out of nowhere. I would turn oars into snakes, wood into ivy. I would make men mad with the sound of my flute. I traveled to the East, founding cities here and there. The nations who did not honor me, I'd make them dry."

"But one day I started aging. Magic wouldn't come out easily anymore. Men forgot my face. And now I just do tricks with coins on the road."

The three women are crying.

"You were great!", says one of them.

"The very best!", shouts another one.

"We all followed your lead!", cries the third.

"It is late", says Mr. Vertigo, melancholic. "We shall better sleep."

That night I have a weird dream. I am lying on the floor, with my eyes open, but can't speak or move. Mr. Vertigo is there, and so are the three women. They are having a heated discussion.

"Forget it!", says Mr. Vertigo.

"I just want to eat his toes!", insists one of the women.

"See the pendant!", says Mr. Vertigo, pointing at my neck. "You can't touch him! That *whore* has marked him!"

"The whore!", shout the three women.

"Look!", one of them says, pointing at me. "He's awake!"

"What?", replies Mr. Vertigo. Everyone is now staring at me. Then I hear the sound of a flute, and everything starts turning around.

XIV

My grandmother the queen Pyrene had been sick for months. Every day her head was getting smaller. Doctors had given her herbal infusions and sucked her blood. Twenty goats had been sacrificed to the god Asclepius. All for nothing: her head had shrunk to the point that servants had to cut chickpeas in half so that they would fit in her tiny mouth. With such a small nose, she couldn't get enough air, so even the shortest walk left her out of breath. All doctors consulted agreed that Pyrene's death was a matter of weeks.

Desperate, my grandfather Antiochus visited the oracle of Delphi. The oracle spoke of a large red flower that only grew in the fields of the island of Seriphos. Only an infusion of that plant could make the queen's head recover its usual size.

Antiochus sent several ships to Seriphos, but none of them returned. In fact, no one in Pleuron had received any news from Seriphos for a year. Sailors told stories of a giant sea monster that dwelled in the banks of the island. The monster, an illegitimate daughter of the god Ares, would destroy any ship from the continent that attempted to reach the island. Her name was Hecate.

Antiochus assigned my father his first task: he was to sail to the island of Seriphos and bring back the red healing flowers.

Diligent, my father rented a boat and recruited a small crew. Just before weighting anchor, though, my father saw Athena walking by the docks. Curious by her presence, my father got off the ship and followed the goddess to a nearby alley. Once alone, Athena spoke:

"Your father has entrusted you a very dangerous mission, and I fear that this time your strength alone might not save you. So I brought you some help."

Athena handed my father a small glass bottle containing a thick black liquid.

"This is the strongest poison I could make. It is enough to kill the Hecate, if you find a way to make her ingest it. A single drop would kill all the fish in the ocean, so please use it with care. Hopefully, you won't need it."

My father put the bottle in one of his inner pockets and thanked Athena.

A few minutes later, he was sailing the Ionian sea.

My father and his crew didn't experience any problem in getting to Seriphos, where they soon found a number of red flowers. When my father and his crew tried to abandon the island, though, a giant black eel surfaced from the depths of the sea and destroyed the ship with a blow of its tail.

As soon as he saw the Hecate, my father swam towards her. He was about to deal the monster a blow, when the Hecate opened her big mouth and my father was sucked inside. He lost consciousness almost immediately.

When my father woke up, he found himself in the middle of a swamp. The whole place smelled of rotten eggs. The ground was covered in black moss, the sun nowhere to be seen. A thick grey mist surrounded everything.

"Am I dead?", thought my father.

In the distance, my father could see the silhouette of a building of some sort. In the absence of a better plan, he started walking towards it.

The building turned out to be a palace, around which many small cottages were scattered. My father walked through fields of wheat and also some herbs and fruits that he didn't recognize. He entered the palace and asked for an audience with the king.

The king was very surprised to meet a new person. Intrigued, he offered my father accommodation in the palace quarters, where my father would spend three days and three nights. During this time, he learned that the people inhabiting the swamp called themselves Atlanteans. They seemed to speak a very archaic form of Greek, and sometimes my father had problems to understand their speech. He also noticed that they didn't have words for "sun", "day", "night" or "sea". When my father told the court that they were living in the stomach of a giant eel, everybody laughed at the idea.

Looking for a way out, my father conducted several expeditions to explore the swamp. In one of his trips, my father discovered a wide river that disappeared under a mountain. Guessing that those waters flowed into the intestine of the sea monster, my father took out the flask of poison that Athena had given him and emptied it in the river.

Soon the earth started shaking, and everything turned dark. Poisoned, the Hecate was emptying the contents of her stomach, Atlantis included. While the monster agonized, my father and most of the Atlanteans swam to the coast of Seriphos.

Thankful to my father for having set them free, the Atlanteans constructed a large ship and brought my father back to Pleuron. Then the Atlanteans sailed West, determined to find a virgin land where they could start a nation.

And what happened to queen Pyrene? With the aid of the red flowers brought by my father, she quickly recovered from her sickness and would live many more decades thereafter.

My father had completed his first labor.

XV

I wake up feeling like shit. My head aches. So do my bowels. The sun is already on the West: I must have slept for the whole day. I look at my arms; they are red from the sun. So must be my face: it burns like crazy. Beside me, there is a pool of vomit.

Mr. Vertigo and his followers are nowhere to be seen, the bonfire just ashes. Uneasy, I sit up. My muscles ache from yesterday's excesses: there's no way I'm exercising today. I put on my sandals, I am ready to resume my trip.

But am I? Something's missing... Carefully, I go through my meagre possessions. My mat, my map, my sandals. Yep, that's all.

Wait, my sword! Where is Diana? Where the hell is my sword? I amble around the bonfire, shouting obscenities, but I can't see the sword anywhere, just hare bones. Fuck.

No time for laments, I already start feeling febrile. I have a sunstroke: I need to find water and a shade. About 200 meters up the road there are some rocks; perhaps there is water, too! Staggering, I follow the path.

Bummer! There is no water. In fact, there is hardly any shade. A large vertical rock projects a tiny shadow over the ground. It is almost midday, so the shade can just cover my feet. Desperate, I take a nearby stone and quickly dig a shallow hole.

I bury my legs and torso, leaving just the arms outside, half-covered by the shade of the rock and some thickets I find around. The cold ground feels so comforting. I try to sleep for some hours, but I just can't: my throat is too dry, it hurts when I breathe.

Then I have a strange idea: I take the Priestess' pendant and put it in my mouth. I explore its surface with my tongue, trying to picture the relief of the warrior woman. The pendant is cool and sweet, and soon I am salivating.

For a spell, I try to guess what the Priestess must be doing right now. I imagine her studying mathematics or writing poetry. Most likely, she already acquired new servants. I hope that she still remembers me.

A bird's tweet wakes me up very early in the morning. I emerge from the hole I dug and beat the dust out of my clothes. The hangover is gone, but I still feel weak. My arms are very red, and their skin has started to peel.

I look at the road. If I go back, I risk getting lynched by the Athenians. I have no choice but continue the trip. But I'm thirsty and hungry, and I don't have any money. More worryingly, I don't have my bow: this means that I can't hunt either.

First things first: I need some sort of breakfast. I amble around, collecting *horta*, the wild greens. I gather dandelion, thistle roots, mustard leaves and sorrel. I sit close to the extinguished bonfire and eat them. They taste fine, but my mouth is too dry to really enjoy them. I'm so thirsty!

I follow the road, stopping from time to time to pick up more *horta*, that I put in my pockets. Like yesterday, the sun is hitting hard. I make myself a sort of hat with some herbs and keep walking up the dusty road. Soon I can't chew any more grass: my tongue feels like leather. Once more, I stick the Priestess' pendant in my mouth.

When I'm thinking that I can't stand the thirst anymore, a miracle. On the right side of the road, in the brightest green, I see a prickly pear! Without hesitation, I run to the plant, that, from afar, looks like one meter tall. While on my way, I imagine the delicious juice touching my lips, and flowing over my tongue to the dry throat.

As I reach the plant, though, reality slaps me on the face. Such a large plant, and it only has three little pieces of fruit! Worse even, they aren't ripe. I tear them off the plant and chew them with the desperation of the damned. After two frustrating minutes, I spit them out: not only they don't have any juice, but they are terribly sour.

The sun is setting again and I feel like a thread-less puppet. I just lie on the ground and pass out, the pendant still in my mouth.

I wake up a few hours later, trembling. My head hurts like crazy, I must have the fever. I stand up and keep walking the road. If I managed to reach a village, I could ask for hospitality, or at least for a bucket of water.

The sun makes my headache worse, but I don't have the energy to cover my skull; I can do nothing but keep walking. I don't bother gathering *horta* anymore, just walk and walk. Everything is turning around, and I am cold, and my muscles ache and I am trembling, and I just want to lie down and close my eyes and meet my father.

Then I notice the leopard.

XVI

The leopard is in the middle of the road, the size of a large wolf. His hair is white and yellow, with black rosettes. He is looking straight at me, his eyes round and yellow.

The leopard and I look at each other for a while. I wonder what the hell a loose leopard is doing in Greece, in this specific road, at 20 meters distance from me.

The leopard just yawns.

"That's a good sign", I think. "It means that he's not hungry. All I have to do is retreat slowly and…"

Coward.

The Harpy's flying over my head.

Coward!

"Leave me alone!", I protest.

Your father…

"Don't! Don't you dare! Shut up!"

Your father is in hell, ashamed of his son!

At first, the leopard just looks at me, confused. When he grasps that I am running *towards him*, the beast jumps back, adopting a defense stance. The lips part, revealing long sharp fangs. The leopard roars, and it sounds like a see-saw. None of that is slowing me down: I am going to beat up the bastard. The leopard is now in attacking position.

All of a sudden, he jumps at me and I close my eyes.

My left arm is in great pain. I open my eyes, to find the leopard standing on its back legs. My arm is up to my elbow inside its mouth. I must have raised it when he jumped.

The leopard tries to aim at my throat with the paws, but his front legs are a bit too short. Then he tries to pull back. I react quickly: before he slips my left arm out of his mouth, I grip his throat with my right hand. He's trapped!

The fucker is biting my arm to the bone, but I keep squeezing his windpipe. Whenever he tries to pull back, I push my left arm deeper into his mouth. And I keep tightening. The leopard contorts, growls and shakes, the leopard tears the skin of my arm with his paws.

But he knows that I'm winning. I am choking the fucker.

At some point, I realize that the leopard is not standing any more: I am lifting his full weight. Nonetheless I keep squeezing for some more time.

The leopard is dead. I take my left arm out of his mouth and the leopard drops. My left arm is a mess: there are two deep holes on my forearm, from which blood flows. I feel exhausted, so I sit on the floor.

During the fight, I didn't feel the fever, the weakness or the thirst. Now it all comes at once: all of a sudden, I'm shivering, I'm dizzy, my head aches.

I'm lying on the floor, in fetal position. It's so cold, and I feel terrible and I want to die and I'm hearing voices.

"Father, over there!"

"What's this?"

"He needs help!"

"Artemis, don't touch him! He could be carrying a plague!"

"Nonsense! Father, help me move him!"

"The leopard! He killed the leopard...!"

The voices grow distant while I fall and fall down the abyss...

XVII

Most of Pleuron's wealth came from its world-famous craftmanship. Every few months, ships full of vases, bowls, marble statuettes, shoes and tinted glasses would cross the Corinthian gulf to reach the ports of Megaris. From that point on, the merchandise was transported by land to different poleis in Eastern Greece. The whole enterprise generated a constant flux of drachmas in the opposite direction, which made Pleuron a very prosperous kingdom.

Lately, though, revenues were getting smaller and smaller. A giant snake that lived near the city of Megara had been attacking the merchants' caravans. The snake, called Iantha, didn't feel fear or pain, and was known to be immortal. Its presence in the road to Megara meant that merchants had to take long detours to deliver Pleuron's crafts to the Eastern cities, with the corresponding price increase. It was a matter of time before Athens or Eleusis improved their craft supply and took over the market.

King Antiochus commanded my father to get rid of the snake. And so began my father's second labor.

My father traveled to Nisaia in a merchant ship. Once in land, he led the pottery caravan towards Megara. After a couple of hours' walk, he and the merchants saw in the distance what looked like a fallen tree. The trunk was copper-colored and it completely blocked the road. When my father came close to remove it from the path, the trunk started slithering.

The trunk was, of course, Iantha's body. The snake quickly disappeared on the bushes on one side of the road, only to reappear, seconds later, in front of my father. The snake had yellow eyes with pupils. Its fangs were long like oars and its mouth was big enough to *swallow a cow. Raising its head to the height of a building, the snake hissed.*

And its sulfur breath blew the bushes away, made the merchants' hair white and hid the sun.

Abandoning the caravan, the merchants run away back to the safety of the docks. My father stayed to face the beast.

And the fight started. First, the snake tried to bite my father, who, rolling over, dodged the attack. Next, my father punched the snake on the jaw. That stunned the snake, but didn't knock it out. The snake tried to attack again, but by then my father had taken out his sword, and dealt the snake a terrible blow on the mouth. The snake must have felt disconcerted: nothing in the last thousand years had managed to make it bleed!

The fight continued for a while, with my father and the snake exchanging blows and bites. By then, my father had beaten the snake badly. He had cut it, strangled it and broken its spine. However, no matter how hard my father stroke, the creature wouldn't die.

Frustrated, my father tied Iantha's tail to a giant rock. Held by its own immortal body, the snake now couldn't attack anyone. However, it was contorting with such ferocity that the whole Earth was shaking.

Hence my father dragged rock and snake to the depths of an abysmal cave near Eleusis and closed the entrance with stones. Whenever there is an earthquake, it is caused by the snake, who keeps trying to break free from the rock that imprisons it.

My father had completed his second labor.

XVIII

I wake up on a very comfortable bed, covered in white blankets which smell of mint and basil. The Priestess' pendant lies on a bedsite table. I am in a small room, with wooden walls and a stone floor.

The shutter of the room's only window has a dent, from which a sunbeam travels across the room, illuminating a pine door. For a while, I contemplate the specks of dust dancing along the beam. I hadn't felt this peaceful in ages.

Some time later, a forty-year-old woman enters the room. She has black hair and a strong face. She's carrying a bucket and some pieces of cloth.

"You're awake!", she says, smiling.

I try to talk back, but my mouth is dry, and my throat hurts, so I end up croaking.

The woman takes a bowl from a shelve above my head. She brings it to my lips.

"There, drink a bit", she says. I comply. The fresh water is sweet like nectar.

I ask the woman who she is.

"My name is Leto", she answers. "My husband and my daughter found you lying on the road, so they brought you to our farm. That was three days ago."

"Thank you", I say. "Thank you very much."

"You're welcome. What is your name, son?"

"I am Thessalus, son of Thasus."

"Nice to meet you, Thasus. Soon you'll meet the rest of my family."

"Not Thasus", I say. "Thess…" I can't complete the sentence, my throat hurts too much.

Leto nods. "You still have the fever. You're a mess!" She starts removing the blankets. "I need to clean your wounds", she explains.

Leto washes my left arm and bandages it with cotton and some roots. She keeps talking in a soothing, sweet voice, and at some point I fall asleep.

The next day I leave the warm comfort of the blankets and stand up. For a moment, everything turns black, but I quickly recover the vision.

The first thing I do is open the window. A garden of grapevines greets my eyes. On my right, a kid of about six plays with a black cat.

"Hello!", I greet him.

Startled, the kid runs back to the house.

I contemplate the view for a while, enjoying the fresh morning air. Then I close the shutter and leave the room.

Soon I am in what appears to be the living room. Leto knits on a chair while she speaks with the boy I saw through the window.

"Thasus!", she exclaims when she sees me. "How do you feel today?"

I'm about to correct her, but I just don't have the energy. "Much better, thanks", I reply.

"My daughter and my husband are now hunting; they will return soon. This is my son, Hermes."

The kid hides behind his mother.

"He's a bit shy", she laughs. "Thasus, sit with me", she says, pointing at a stool beside her. I oblige.

"We're all working very hard, lately", she says, tired, while she resumes her knitting. "We plow, we hunt, we sell craftmanship… but we can hardly cope with the taxes."

"Don't you have slaves?"

"Not any more", she says. "We sold the last one a year ago to pay the Lord."

"A yearly slave? That's a very high levy!"

"It is! The Old Lord, may he rest in peace, was a just ruler. He took the exact amount he needed to pay his army and keep the polis going. And he built bridges and roads and wells. Those were the good times: there was hard work, yes, but we also had time for dancing. But ever since the Old Lord died..." She sighs and shakes her head.

"His son Keres is different. He just wants to waste our drachmas in extravagancies."

"Extravagancies? Like...?"

"Like the leopard that almost ate you!", she replies. "It escaped a few weeks ago from the Lord's palace. Everyone here was so scared of taking that road!"

"How... how did you kill the leopard?", asks Hermes, timidly.

"I suffocated him."

"With your hands?"

"Yes."

"Were you scared?"

"No." Leto smiles, but says nothing.

The kid is staring at me, his mouth open. I know that look very well. I also looked at my father that way.

The door opens and a heavyset man enters the home. He wears a grey tunic and a thick well-groomed squared beard. He smiles when he sees me.

"Our guest has awaken!", he says, approaching me. I stand up and we shake hands. "I am Zeus", he says.

"I am Thessalus. Thank you very much for saving me, Sir", I say. "I owe you my life."

"Oh, it wasn't me who found you, Thasus". He looks at the open door. "Artemis! You'll clean your arrows later. Come and meet our visitor!"

A maiden enters, carrying a dead hare tied to her waist. She doesn't wear a dress, but a man's linen tunic. She has strong calves and biceps, wide hips, thick lips and big brown eyes. Her long black hair falls like a cascade till her waist. She also looks my age.

We are both still, glaring at each other. She smiles timidly, the prettiest smile I've ever seen. I smile back. I can feel my cheeks, nose and forehead reddening.

Leto's laugh ruins everything. Artemis frowns at her, annoyed and embarrassed. With a curt apology, she leaves the room.

"Don't worry", Leto tells me. "She'll come back." She laughs out loud. Out of the corner of my eye, I see Zeus restraining his laughter.

Things get a little bit less awkward when we all sit for lunch. Leto serves us a rabbit stew with horta and some cheese. Artemis is sitting opposite to me, looking at her plate.

"So, Thasus, what brought you to these lands?", Zeus asks.

"I'm on my way to mount Olympus", I reply.

"Mount Olympus? What a ridiculous destination! Why would anyone go to mount Olympus?"

"I'm meeting someone", I answer.

I don't want to explain my mission, they wouldn't understand. Even worse, they would think I'm nuts.

"Crazy! There's nothing in mount Olympus!", Zeus says.

Leto intervenes. "Zeus, leave the poor kid alone!". She addresses me. "Thasus, tell us something about you."

I look at Artemis. This is my chance to shine! I proudly recount my adventures fighting bandits, my trial and my escape from Athens. And, of course, my brave combat against the leopard.

"... I was on the verge of fainting when I heard an extremely sweet voice in distress, alerting her father. How could I imagine that I was going to be saved by such an enchanting maiden?", I conclude, looking straight at Artemis...

... who rolls her eyes. With an expression of boredom mixed with disgust, Artemis excuses herself and leaves the living room.

Damn. I overdid it! Sighing, I look around. Leto has returned to her knitting, Zeus is distracted trying to remove something from between his teeth. Hermes, on the other hand, is looking at me, ecstatic.

I don't dislike admiration, but the kid's glare is a bit too much to bear. Uncomfortable, I look around the room. Then my eyes set on a familiar metallic shape leaning against one of the corners of the room.

"My sword!", I shout.

I get close and hold it. Yes, there's no doubt. This is Diana.

"Where did you find it?"

Zeus looks confused. "A group of beggars sold me the sword. That was four days ago".

"An old man with three old women?"

"No", he says. "They were a man and three women, but they weren't old. The man was in his thirties; the women looked much younger."

"What are you talking about?", interrupts Leto. "The man was at least seventy. And none of the women had teeth!"

Hermes intervenes. "They were teenagers. I thought that they had run away from home."

"In any case", says Zeus, "I paid a lot for this sword, Thasus. Are you sure it's yours?"

"This was my father's sword", I explain. "It was stolen from me by these four people, my cellmates in Athens."

"Could it be that your sword was the price to help you escape?".

"No way. The sword was never part of any deal. They stole it while I was asleep, then left for good." I am getting angry.

Leto steps in. "Ah, Zeus! Give the kid back his sword!"

"I can't! I was counting on reselling it to pay our taxes!" He looks at me, conflicted.

This man saved my life, he gave me hospitality when I needed it the most. But I must get that sword back.

"I will pay you", I say.

"How? You didn't carry a single obol when we found you. I checked."

Leto stares at Zeus, disapproving. Zeus shrugs.

"I will pay you with my work. Leto says that you don't have slaves, that all of you are working your asses to meet the Lord's taxes."

"That's right", mutters Zeus. He is interested.

"In exchange for food and a bed, I will work for you until I have earned the price of that sword."

Zeus ponders my proposal. "The price I paid for the sword or the price I intended to charge for it?"

"The second", I say.

"But you don't know how much money I expected to earn. I could fool you right now."

"You saved me. You are an honorable man. I trust you."

Zeus smiles.

"I like this boy!"

"So, deal?"

"Deal. Now, let's go to the tavern. An agreement between two men counts for nothing if not sworn in front of an amphora of good red wine."

"Er... OK...", I mumble, feeling a pang of nausea.

"Can I come too?", asks Hermes.

"Sure!", replies Zeus. "A tavern is a place as good as any to raise a five-year old."

XIX

"Of course, I was being ironic", says Zeus to his son. "I didn't really mean you to come with us."

"Bampás! I am too young to spot irony!", replies Hermes laughing.

"He's so witty, my son", says Zeus, stroking Hermes' hair.

The three of us are in the town's tavern. We are sitting on one side of a large rectangular table. The wood is very dark, and covered with wax, or something else just as sticky.

All of a sudden, Hermes shouts: "Homer, Homer!!" Hermes is greeting at a ten-year-old who ambles in the bar. He is pale and thin, with blond hair.

The kid comes to our table. He returns the greeting:

"Hello, little Hermes! Is your father with you?"

"Yes, I am!", replies Zeus. "And we come with a guest. On my right there's young Thasus, from Tyria."

"May I join you?", asks Homer. Not waiting for an answer, he sits next to me.

"Nice to meet you", I say, extending my hand.

Homer also extends his hand, but doesn't grab mine.

"You're not very quick, Thasus", says Homer.

It finally strikes me: Homer is blind! Embarrassed, I shake his hand.

"What are you doing in this town?", asks Homer.

"I'll work for Zeus for a while, then I'm heading North."

"To Mount Olympus!", adds Hermes.

"Speaking of which", says Homer, "did you know that Mount Olympus is inside a cliff?"

"What?"

"Mount Olympus is the tallest mountain in the world. However, since its base sits on a very deep well, one just needs to jump a few meters in order to climb to the top."

"Thasus, don't believe anything that Homer says", intervenes Zeus, "He lies through his teeth!"

"I'm serious!", protests Homer. "In fact, I've heard that in the depth of mount Olympus foothills, lives a race of blind Titans. Their skin is white as salt, and they devour whomever falls from the cusp of the mountain."

Homer speaks for some time about Titans, gods and monsters. But Hermes is getting impatient: he has something important to tell!

"Homer!", he bursts, interrupting Homer's story. "Thasus is the man who killed the leopard!"

"What? Is this true? You killed the Lord's leopard?"

"Yes, I…"

"Father! Father!"

The man behind the bar leaves his workplace and comes to our table. He is fat and bald, and has a gentle expression. He places his thick hand on Homer's shoulders.

"What's the matter, son?"

"Father!", he says, pointing more or less in my direction. "This is the man who killed the fearsome leopard!"

"You're the hero who freed us from that beast?", he asks. Zeus nods, and the bartender shakes my hand. Then he addresses the bar. "Hey!", he shouts. "Silence everybody!"

Everyone shuts up.

"What's your name, son?", he whispers.

"I am Thessalus, son of Thasus."

"Listen everyone! This is Thasus. Three days ago, this badass killed the Lord's panther with his own hands!"

Everybody awes and gasps.

"Irene!", he shouts. "Bring the craft!"

Soon, a mature thick woman abandons the kitchen and approaches our table. She carries something in her hands, that she hands to the bartender. The latter speaks again.

"When Zeus told me that a foreign youngster had killed the creature who had terrorized us for weeks, I couldn't wait to go shake his hand. For the whole village had suffered with me. For weeks, we couldn't sell or buy any goods. Not even the bravest merchants dared come to Nephele!"

Everyone nods, approvingly.

"But Zeus told us that you were badly hurt, he feared for your life! Since I couldn't meet you, I decided to make you a present. So I went to the road, found the carcass of that evil monster... and made this!"

The bartender extends the piece of cloth that he was holding against his belly. It is the leopard's skin!

"Young Thasus", the bartender says, while handing me the skin. "The town of Nephele salutes you!"

The bar customers clap wildly. I don't know what to do, so I stand up and put the skin around my shoulders. And then everyone stands up too, and come to meet us. And we drink and we talk, and we shout and we get to know each other.

Hours later, at night, when the party mood is starting to decay, everyone suddenly falls silent. Three men, dressed as soldiers, have just entered the tavern.

Two of them stand very close to our table. The third one, very proud and confident, slowly walks up to the bar. Everyone is holding their breath. I can smell their fear.

"What happens?", he says, looking at the customers with the smile of a hyena. "Why is everyone so quiet in this bar? I understand, we all have problems and regrets. Bartender!", he greets, "how are things going?"

"Well, Captain, the business is a bit weak these days", the bartender replies, with a nervous laugh. He doesn't look cheerful and charming anymore.

"But I see a lot of people around", the Captain replies.

"Today is a bit special, Sir. But these last weeks..."

The Captain cuts him short. "Just give me my money, bartender."

"Yes, Sir", the bartender says.

He searches below the bar and produces a handful of coins. The Captain counts them and then stares at the bartender for some seconds.

"There must be something in my eye, bartender. I only see twenty drachmas on the bar."

"That's all I earned this week, Sir. Next week, though…"

"That's what you said last week." He snaps his fingers.

Grabbing Homer by the throat, one of the soldiers pulls him from his stool and drags him to the bar. I'm about to intervene, but Zeus holds me. I look at him and he shakes his head. He's scared shitless.

The Captain produces a small dagger and puts it at Homer's neck. Homer jumps when the blade touches his skin.

"Can you feel what this is, Homer?"

"Please, Sir!", implores the bartender. "He's just a child!"

"I'm not talking to you!", shouts the Captain. He turns back to Homer. "Homer, answer the question. What is touching your neck?"

"A knife", says Homer.

"Very good, Homer", says the Captain. "Bartender, what price would you put to your boy's neck? Another twenty drachmas, perhaps?"

"Sir, I don't have any more money. Please put the knife down."

"Don't tell me how to do my job!"

"Sorry, Sir. Please leave my child alone, Sir. I'll pay you double next week, I promise. We just don't have all the money now…"

"I understand, my good man. I am not a heartless soldier! What kind of monster would kill a boy for twenty drachmas? Your boy's life is worth much more."

The bartender looks at him with suspicion.

"So I'll tell you what we'll do", says the Captain." If you don't produce twenty more drachmas right now, I'm going to empty your boy's right eye socket. Not that he has much use for it!", he laughs. "Next week, if you haven't managed to gather 60 drachmas, I'll empty your boy's left socket. On the third week, we'll reconsider the terms of this deal."

Irene kneels before the leader.

"Please, Sir! Don't harm my child!"

"You have three seconds to hand the rest of the levy", says the Captain. "Three."

The Harpy caws:

Coward.

She's perching on a chair, close to the Captain.

The Captain starts moving his dagger towards Homer's eye.

"Two."

You will not intervene because you have no guts. You are the shame of your family, you are your father's shame. You don't deserve to live, you poor...

"Sir! I beg you! We don't have the money!"

Homer is tightening the eyelids.

"Homer, cooperate", says the Captain, opening Homer's eye with his left hand.

... will watch them mutilate the child. Because that's what you do, watch. You won't fight, no! All that training and now you're shitting your pants! Just like that time when your...

"One."

"Leave the kid alone."

That's me, speaking. I'm standing up in the middle of the room. I mustn't look very threatening, with my skin full or bruises and my left arm in a cast.

The Captain turns around.

"Excuse me?"

"If you don't let the kid go *now*, I'm going to tear your balls off and have you watch how these two retards eat them."

For a response, the Captain turns around and, facing Homer, lifts his dagger...

"I'll give you thirty more drachmas!", shouts the bartender.

"What?"

The bartender opens a compartment on a barrel, and a few coins drop.

"This money, we use it to buy supplies. Without it, we are broke. Take it. Take it all."

Irene is looking at the floor, crying.

Reluctant, the Captain leaves Homer and pockets all the money.

"What about him?", he says, pointing at me.

The Harpy has abandoned the chair. It is hovering in front of me, half a meter from my face.

For a moment, I thought that you'd do it, I thought that you'd behave like a man. But you can't, can you? Because you're not a man. You're a rabbit. You're a weak little rabbit who would betray his own...

I walk toward the soldiers. They draw their swords and adopt a defensive position.

"That boy is completely drunk!", shouts the bartender. "He didn't mean it! Right, Thasus?"

He's looking at me with desperation. So is everyone else.

... make me puke. You suck. You should have been born dead. We would all be...

"Yes", I reply. "I don't know what I say. Sorry for my unfortunate remark."

The soldiers sheathe their swords.

"Are you really sorry?", asks the Captain.

"I am, Sir."

"Then kneel down and apologize."

Coward! Coward! Coward!

Everyone looks at me. They are all frightened.

I kneel down.

"I am sorry."

"Good!", he says, and kicks me hard on the head.

For a moment, I see the stars. I quickly recover my vision, but my head hurts like crazy. While I moan on the floor, I see the Captain and his men abandoning the bar. The party is over.

Zeus, Hermes and I walk silently back to the farm. Just before we enter his home, Zeus halts and tells me:

"If you had confronted those men tonight, the Lord's army would have come to town in the morning. And they would have killed us all."

XX

Zeus puts me in charge of one of the fields beyond the grapevines. For the next months, I work like I have never worked before. I plow the land, plant spinach, carrots, green beans. I work from sunrise till sunset. No matter how much energy I put, there is always something else to do. By the end of the day, I'm so tired that I just collapse on my bed.

Later, things improve. Since the crops I have planted just need some watering in the evening, Zeus puts me to pasture the goats. I am no longer exhausted. In fact, most evenings, Zeus and I pay a visit to the tavern. Thanks to donations, the bartender has managed to keep the business afloat.

The extra time also gives me the chance to resume my combat training. My arms heal quickly, but they have turned weak. I start an intensive workout program that involves handstands over the backs of my hands, one-legged jumping squats and one-armed pushups with my legs up against a tree. Slowly, I recover my tone.

Something else is happening too. My body is becoming wider, much more muscled than before. My voice turns an octave lower, a thick brown beard grows on my face. I catch a few of the town's women staring at me.

But the beautiful Artemis doesn't take notice. Every time I talk to her, the conversation turns awkward. I soon run out of things to say, she always looks so bored.

To hell with her, I give up.

A week later, Artemis reaches me. I have some free time, so I am throwing arrows against a tree.

"Thasus", she starts, "is there anything wrong?"

"No. Why?"

"Well, you aren't talking to me lately."

"Do you think?", I reply, while shooting an arrow.

"Are you avoiding me?"

"Not at all", I reply. I shoot another arrow.

"Then come with me. We're going hunting."

"Nay. I'd rather stay here practicing my aim", I say, shooting my last arrow.

"Can I try?", she asks.

"Be my guest."

Artemis unhangs her bow and loads one of her arrows. She aims carefully and... thwack!

Her arrow has impinged, not only on the tree, but on one of my own arrows! Astonished, I run to the tree. Artemis' arrow is well stuck in the bark. My arrow lies cracked open on the floor.

"How did you...?"

"Farming is boring", she says behind me, "and Dad doesn't let me go to the tavern. Since I was five, I haven't done anything but hunting."

"You don't like knitting, like your mother?"

"That's for girls".

She removes her arrow from the tree and holds my arm tightly. I start.

"Listen, Thasus!", she says, abruptly. "Shooting at a still target won't improve your aim much further. Let's go shoot hares. The fuckers run like the wind."

Who could resist such charms? I follow her like a puppy.

Once in the wild, there's not much for me to do, except looking at how Artemis kills every single rat, partridge or hare crossing our way. Her technique is perfect. She moves with amazing grace and stealth, sometimes climbing trees in order to find a more advantageous spot to take her prey. Sometimes, she chases the game through the undergrowth, all the time shooting arrows at her unfortunate prey.

When we get tired of hunting, Artemis and I check her traps. We retrieve a thrush from under a heavy rock and a live goldfinch trapped in birdlime. At some point, she is explaining me how to make a rabbit trap with a lasso. By then I can hardly pay attention. She is so exceptional and pretty! I just want to jump on her and grab her thin waist and kiss her thick red lips!

Artemis and I are now sitting on a hill, with a full view of Nephele. Our bounty –four hares and six birds— lies on the grass in front of us.

A few white constructions some kilometers west of the town attract my attention.

"What are those buildings?", I ask.

"Those are the Lord's headquarters", she replies. "This is where Lord Keres thinks of new, innovative ways to waste our money."

"Is that a theater?"

"Yes, it is. When the Old Lord ruled, there were theater festivals and concerts once or twice a year. The whole town would gather there! There were musicians, acrobats and comedians. It was so funny…!"

For a moment, she's lost in her thoughts. Then her mood changes.

"The new Lord put an end to all that", she says, bitter.

"He stopped organizing activities?"

"No. The best musicians and comedians in Greece perform in the theater year after year. But the citizens of Nephele are no longer allowed to enter. The Lord is the only spectator."

"What? Why?"

"Because he doesn't want to mix with us, ignorant peasants! He just wants to squeeze us dry. We haven't seen him in years, the fool, always locked up in his stupid palace."

After that, she is pensive for some time.

I change the subject:

"Artemis, this was so impressive!", I say, pointing at the game. "If you put your mind to it, you could extinguish the local fauna in three or four days."

She laughs. "Do you think?"

"I do! You're an incredible hunter! I had never seen anything like you!"

"Thanks", she says, smiling.

Next there's a long silence.

I don't know what else to say. Shall I kiss her? But, how? We are one meter apart!

"Let's go back home", she says at last.

Damn.

We stand up and start walking. She looks disappointed, or at least that's what I think. None of us speaks until the farm is on sight.

Three soldiers are standing on the yard. Zeus is outside the house, discussing with one of them. As we get close, I see that it's the soldier who caused the incident in the bar.

Zeus is saying: "I just need some more time; what you demand is not reasonable."

"Are you saying that the Lord's orders are unreasonable?", asks the Captain.

Artemis and I are now standing next to Zeus. No one is paying attention to us. From the house's front window, little Hermes is peeking at the scene.

"I am just saying that those time demands can't be met", says Zeus. "I need another week. If you give me another week, then I can sell a couple of things."

I fear what one of those things will be.

"I've had a lot of patience with you, old peasant", says the Captain. Then he notices Artemis. "Oh! What do we have here? Why don't you sell me *this*?"

The Captain takes Artemis' hand. "Look at her, guys!", he says, pointing at her hips and breasts. "Zeus, where does this beautiful nymph come from? Not from your balls, I presume". He chuckles. "Like a gazelle and a weasel…"

The Captain then *grabs* Artemis' chin.

I can't move, I can't breathe. My vision is clouded and my heart is beating very fast.

"What's wrong, baby? Did you swallow something hard?". The other soldiers laugh.

The Harpy is perching on the windowsill, next to Hermes. Staring.

Meanwhile, the Captain has left Artemis. Grabbing Zeus' tunic, he throws him to the ground.

"You. fucking. weasel!", the Captain shouts, while he kicks Zeus on the ribs. "If you don't pay your levies by next week, the boys and I will come for your daughter!".

The Harpy is now standing on the floor, to the left of Zeus and the Captain.

Coward.

I start towards the two men, when someone grabs my hand. It's Artemis. She looks at me in the eye and shakes his head.

"We will seriously fuck her up, Zeus! We will pump your daughter so hard that her eyes will pop out!"

Coward! Coward! You coward!

Artemis hasn't let go of my hand. Her hand is soft and warm. For a moment I forget about everything else, cherishing this intimate contact.

The Captain gives Zeus another warning and the soldiers leave the farm.

Zeus stands up and cleans the dust off his tunic. Pointing at the soldiers, he grins like it's not a big deal.

Artemis approaches him slowly, with a compassionate smile, her arms extended. But then Zeus' grin leaves his face and he gestures Artemis to stop. This man doesn't want a hug, he wants to dig a hole and hide. Lost in his thoughts, Zeus enters the house.

I hear Hermes shouting:

"Bampás, bampás!"

Artemis turns around, she's crying. I hug her and she hugs me back. We stand like that for a while.

All of a sudden, she grabs my hand and drags me to the shed.

As soon as we cross the door, she kisses me. On my cheek, on my eyes, on my ears. She hugs me hard and bites my neck.

I grab her chin and kiss her lips.

We lie on the floor, covered with straw. We hug, we roll and kiss again.

I start opening her dress, but she pushes me away.

"What are you doing?"

I don't know what to answer, so I just stare at her.

"Sorry, I shouldn't have started." She stands up and straightens her dress. Without a word, she leaves the shed.

So there I am, alone in the shed with a massive hard-on.

It seems that I need to take matters into my own hands.

XXI

Zeus and I are drinking wine in the tavern. He's been looking pensive for a while. Suddenly, he turns to me. His eyes are closed.

"Thasus", he says. "I'm not giving you back your sword."

"I knew it!", I shout. This is my fourth bowl, and I am completely pissed. "Fucking hell, I knew it!"

"I'm sorry!", he says. I can see that he means it, so I try to calm down.

"I thought that I could gather enough drachmas to appease the Lord's men", he continues, "but there's no way we can meet the deadline. Sorry, Thasus, but I need to sell it."

"Fuck!"

Now we both look pensive.

Homer approaches our table.

"Zeus! Thasus! You're not drinking!"

"What? How do you know?"

"My father asked me to come by. He doesn't like when people don't drink. Thinks it's bad for business." He sits with us. "So what's up, guys?"

"Taxes", answers Zeus.

"Ah!", replies Homer, upset.

The three of us look pensive.

"Zeus", starts Homer, "what happened to the cow?"

"I guess she's still around."

"What cow?"

Homer turns to me, delighted.

"Many years ago, Zeus traveled to Trachis to buy a cow. Unfortunately, he spent most of his money in booze and women."

"Hey!", complains Zeus.

"When Zeus arrived at the market, he just had seven obols left. But no one would sell him a cow for seven miserable obols. He was about to return home and be beaten by his wife…"

"Homer! I am still here!", says Zeus.

"… when he bumped into an old lady who was selling a white cow. The cow was very fat, her udders full of milk. When Zeus asked the lady for a price, the lady asked back:"

"'How much do you carry?'".

"And Zeus replied:"

"'I'm afraid that I just have two obols.'"

"To Zeus' surprise", continued Homer, "the lady agreed to the transaction, and obols and cow exchanged hands."

"However, unbeknown to Zeus, the old lady who had sold him the cow was actually Hera, Zeus' old lover, in disguise."

"That's not true!", protested Zeus.

"Ah, Zeus! What do you know? You were completely drunk!"

"Does he always talk to you like that?", I ask Zeus.

"He grew up in a tavern", replies Zeus philosophically.

"Anyway", resumes Homer, "Zeus' new cow, that he named Europa, was incredibly docile: she graciously let Zeus lead her all the way back to Nephele. After leaving her in the stable, Zeus spent the whole evening boasting to Leto and young Artemis about how he bargained with the vendor to acquire such a nice exemplar."

"The next morning, when Zeus went to milk Europa, he found a completely different animal. To begin, the cow's skin was no longer white, but it had some black spots. As it turned out, Hera had painted the cow in white, and now the paint was detaching. In reality, the cow's whole fur was black like charcoal. More worryingly, the cow didn't look docile and quiet anymore. She was, in fact, a wild beast!"

"The cow would kick Zeus whenever he tried to milk her. She horned a horse, she ate the crops. She pooed in front of the house's main entrance, not because she felt like it, but just to make a point.

Since no shepherd was brave enough to milk or take Europa to the meadows, Zeus decided to turn her into delicious steaks."

"So Zeus started fattening her. He chained her to the stable, fed her grass with a fork and gave her water in a bucket hanging from a long stick. Soon she got large like a whale. One day, Zeus heard a loud crack outside the house."

"It was Europa. She had destroyed the stable and was roaming free on Zeus' fields!"

"Zeus tried to capture her, but Europa was so aggressive and scary that, on second thoughts, he and his family locked themselves inside the house until the cow lost interest. For two days, Europa was mooing at and horning everything within her reach. Zeus didn't leave his home and no villager dared approach Zeus' farm. When Europa devoured the last of Zeus' crops, she trotted off to the mountains."

"Did that really happen?", I ask Zeus.

"Don't judge me! She was not a cow, she was a Chthonic beast! You should have seen her big red eyes!", says Zeus.

"What happened to Europa?", I ask.

"Europa settled in a nearby mountain of mysterious origins that we Nephelians call 'The Eye of Tartarus.'"

"It's called 'The Chicken Peak'", says Zeus, "and there's nothing mysterious about it. In fact, it has very good meadows. Before Europa settled there, many shepherds brought cattle to the Chicken Peak. It's quite close, it was very convenient!"

"Thasus, you must capture Europa, the Cthonic Cow!", concludes Homer.

"What? Why should I?", I ask.

"You are a hero", says Homer, "therefore you must do heroic deeds. I'm just giving you ideas!"

"I'm not a hero!", I protest. "I just want to recover my sword and resume my journey!"

Zeus intervenes: "actually, it's not such a bad idea". I look at him, incredulous.

"The cow is dreadful, sure", says, Zeus, "but she looks like a good catch. If we could get hold of her, then we could pull Hera's trick again: we paint her white, we drug her with mandragora to calm her down and then we hand her to the Lord's men. And all my tax problems will be over!"

The three of us burst laughing. We chat excitedly, we interrupt each other with funny remarks, we drink and shout and sing until the small hours. It's a crazy plan, but it would be so great to get back at those assholes!

There's just one little detail. I need to capture a wild cow.

XXII

Two days later, I'm traveling to the Chicken Peak. My two strongest goats are coming along. They help me pull a wheeled sled, built in half a day by Nephele's master carpenter. Zeus thinks my plan crazy, but I am not afraid. Actually, I feel strangely calm, but also very awake.

Europa is not difficult to find: her black fur stands out in the green of Chicken Peak's meadows. When I spot her chewing grass a few kilometers away, I tie the goats to a nearby tree and silently set up my trap.

Then I go to meet the Chthonic Cow.

On first sight, Europa stares at me, defiant. She has red eyes and is large like a buffalo. When Europa realizes that I'm walking towards her, she starts mooing and *screaming*. She sounds like a crazy bear, I have never heard anything like that!

I run away as soon as she charges.

First thing about cows: it doesn't matter how fast you are, they will always outrun you.

The sound of Europa's hoofs is getting louder and louder. I have nearly reached my trap, so I make a sharp turn to the right and soon another to the left. Europa can't keep up; she falls and rolls on the ground.

Second thing about cows: they are very bad at changing directions.

I am at 200 meters from Europa. She looks at me for a second, then charges again. This time I don't flee. But I don't intend to fight, either.

Third thing about cows: no matter how strong you are, cows are stronger. It is pointless to just go and punch a cow.

Europa has already covered most of the distance. Her horns are aiming at my chest. When she is twenty meters away, I start running *towards* her. I leap high, my right foot landing on her head; my left foot, on her back; and my right foot back on the floor. I have dodged Europa's attack!

The cow runs some more meters down the mountain before realizing that she hasn't hit me. She turns around, frustrated, and charges again.

I smile sympathetically, the poor thing. If she had some sense, she would just leave me alone.

One thing about humans: we have more stamina than any animal or monster. We can work the fields from dawn till sunset. We can climb a mountain, we can cross a desert. We can chase a gazelle for weeks until it drops dead from exhaustion. What we humans can't defeat, we *tire*.

I spend the next half an hour resisting Europa's attacks. I roll away, flip and run. Grabbing Europa's horns, I do a perfect handstand and land safely behind the cow. I cart-wheel away from her, I jump over her as I would jump over a vaulting horse. And little by little, Europa's attacks become slower and her anger lessens.

When Europa can hardly breathe, I lead her to the trap. By then she is not trotting anymore; she just staggers behind me. She's on the brink of fainting.

The trap is on a slope. As soon as Europa enters the lasso that I had left over some stones, I pull the rope with all my strength.

The lasso binds Europa's legs together, and she falls right on the wheeled sled. I use the rest of the rope to tie her to the wooden artifact. Europa doesn't even resist: she's too tired.

I pick up my two goats and we three pull the sled down the mountain. Europa weights like a stone, but I reckon that we can arrive at Nephele by the evening.

Everything went according to plan.

XXIII

Antiochus had spent the day listening to merchants complaining. Some weeks ago, a winged horse had nested in the outskirts of Pleuron; he had probably emigrated from Thessaly to escape a cold winter. The pegasus, that Pleuronians had named Boreas, had been attacking everyone roaming his nest.

Unfortunately, Boreas' nest was near the road that connected Pleuron and Calydon, the closest big polis. Several Locrian merchants who had entered Pleuron by land found themselves trapped in the city, without the possibility to return to their homes. Most worryingly, the transit of crops from the eastern cities had been interrupted. Pleuron's land was barren; with the eastern road closed, the city would soon exhaust its food supplies. Then Antiochus would have to start evacuating his people by the sea…

Antiochus sent several archers to take down Boreas. They came back covered with bruises. The creature was just too fast: you would see it flying far away, dancing with the sun. You blinked, and the creature was in front of you, ready to kick your skull.

Seeing his army unable to deal with the problem, Antiochus asked my father to get rid of the pegasus.

So began my father's third labor.

My father's first encounter with the pegasus didn't go well. He was a great shooter, but the pegasus always managed to dodge his arrows. Neither could my father defeat Boreas in melee combat. A single punch from my father would have crushed the pegasus' head. But Boreas was like a fly: no matter how fast my father hit, the pegasus would avoid every blow.

Boreas kicked my father for half an hour: he ended the fight by defecating on my father's head. Then, with a loud neigh, he flew back to his nest.

"Revenge!", shouted my father, his face covered in horse manure. "Revenge!"

When my father returned all wounded to the palace, he found goddess Athena waiting for him at the gates. She was very surprised to see his poor state.

"Thasus!", she exclaimed. "Did you fight a Titan?"

My father explained Athena his predicament, and asked for her advice to catch the pegasus. Athena pondered for a moment, then said:

"A few kilometers away, just past those hills over there, there is a large meadow. I want you to go there this evening, just before the sunset. Find a nice spot, lay on the green grass and wait silently until it gets dark. Perhaps you'll find some inspiration."

That night, my father went to the meadow and lied on the grass. The cicadas were having a concert, but, as soon as the sun set, everything turned quiet. The moon shone with intensity, and fireflies fluttered all over the place.

Soon two figures came from the city. One of them was an old man with a long beard; the other one, a boy of about 15. None of them noticed my father.

The old man, clearly an alchemist, explained his teenage assistant that he needed fireflies to prepare some potion. He asked the boy to catch as many as he could and keep them in a bottle. To help him catch them, the old man handed the boy a small net on a hoop.

Whenever the boy saw a bunch of fireflies, he would swoop the net at them. The fireflies, all dizzy, their little wings tangled in the net, could not just fly away. The boy would then stick his hand in the net, grab them and place them in the bottle.

In the space of an hour, my father watched the boy catch hundreds of fireflies. Thoughtful, he left the meadow in silence.

The next morning, my father returned to the road to Calydon. He was carrying a drum and a gigantic fishing net. My father extended the net on the ground and tied some weights on its borders. Then he covered the net with some bushes and, leaving the net behind him, started playing the drum loudly.

Awakened by the racket, Boreas left his nest and saw my father in the distance. Thinking that he didn't risk anything, he confidently flew towards my father.

Boreas stopped mid-air at a dozen meters from my father. He probably wondered why the bushes behind my father had such a strange, circular shape. In that moment, my father kicked the drum away, grabbed the tip of the net from behind, and, with a loud laugh, turned the net around over the pegasus.

The net was hundreds of meters wide, leaving Boreas no free path to escape. The net's lead weights fell on the floor. Pushed by the net, Boreas landed heavily on the ground. My father quickly jumped over Boreas and reduced him, tying his wings with a chain.

My father could have killed Boreas on the spot. He could have strangled him with his strong arms, he could have crushed his skull with his hands. He could have kicked and punched the animal to death.

But he didn't. My father had recognized in Boreas a kindred spirit. A creature that had grown too powerful for his own sake, and who desperately needed someone even mightier to mentor him.

Hence my father dedicated the next few weeks to domesticate the pegasus. With my father's chain in place, Boreas could no longer fly, so there was no risk that the animal escaped and caused havoc. Every day my father would ride Boreas from dawn till dusk. The Pegasus resisted: he would bite and kick, he would jump and writhe to shake my father off his back. But my father was stronger, he always had the upper hand.

They didn't fight all the time. Twice a day, my father would speak softly to the animal and give him water and food. At night, when Boreas did not have an iota of strength left in him, my father would lie on the meadow, his head resting on the beast's side. They would both fall asleep looking at the stars.

That's how, day by day, my father won Boreas' trust.

One morning, my father unchained Boreas. Excited, the pegasus tried to fly. But his wings were out of shape, so he fell on the ground. Boreas tried again: first, he galloped a few meters: when he gained speed, he extended his wings fully. He flew some meters high, but very soon lost altitude and landed.

In his third attempt, Boreas flew up into the sky. He flew in spirals, he went up and down, he made pirouettes. He was euphoric!

Then my father called him.

Boreas stopped short. He was hovering, contemplating my father from above. He could go down and meet my father. Or he could fly away and disappear.

My father was uneasy. He called Boreas again.

After a moment of vacillation, Boreas slowly descended, landing in front of my father. My father approached him and gently caressed the animal's forehead. The pegasus neighed happily. Boreas' training had concluded.

That day, the subjects of Pleuron saw something truly remarkable. A man with a winged golden helmet flew over the city gates on a pegasus. Rider and beast fluttered over the marketplace, over the clay workshops, over the temples and monuments of Pleuron. They skillfully descended on the palace gardens, where the king and queen were taking a walk.

Antiochus and Pyrene couldn't believe their eyes. Without a word, my father dismounted Boreas and led the pegasus to the royal stables.

The fact that my father had decided not to kill the beast, but to tame it, convinced king Antiochus that his son had changed for the better, and that he was ready to succeed him. He abdicated on my father the very next day.

My father had completed his last labor.

XXIV

I reach the farm by four. There's nobody around. Then I remember that Leto told me that tonight there is a wine festival: she and her family must be celebrating in Nephele.

So I leave the goats in the farm and, pulling Europa's carriage, head for the town. By then, Europa has recovered her strength, and tries, unsuccessfully, to get rid of her tethers.

My entrance in Nephele's main street is epic.

There I am, a muscled young man pulling alone the sled where the feared one-ton Europa, the horror of Nephele, is mooing and contorting. Pulling the rope with all my strength, my body at a 45-degree angle, I drag the sled at a pace of ten meters per minute, all the time looking at the floor.

A crowd of Nephelians are shouting, laughing and patting me on the back. They have been following me since I met them in the outskirts of the town.

The people in the main street, all wearing costumes and carrying bowls of wine, have stopped singing. They can't believe their eyes. It must look like a scene out of a relief.

"What's going on?", asks Homer, who stands with some adults in front of the tavern.

While they explain him, I halt the sled in front of Zeus and Artemis, who are also near the tavern, speechless as everyone else.

"Well, Zeus, there you are", I say. "Next time, ask for something *really* difficult."

Zeus gets close to the sled and feels Europa's side. The black cow moos and growls, she spits foam and tries to bite Zeus' hand. She's really furious, but the rope keeps her still.

Grabbing my shoulder, Zeus looks at me straight in the eye. He nods and smiles, he's satisfied.

Everybody starts clapping.

Soon everything turns crazy. Some youngsters lift me up in the air. They parade me through the street, as if I were some god's wood carving. And the people shout: "Thasus, Thasus, Thasus, Thasus…!"

The parade dies, but not the festival. Everyone is singing or playing the crotalum. Somehow, a bowl of wine has materialized in my hand. Everybody wants to talk to me. I chat with men, women, boys and girls. The girls touch their hair and shrink their stomachs. They look at me with very wide eyes.

When I see Artemis leaving the festival, I go after her.

I catch her in a quiet and dark road.

"Hello, Artemis!", I say.

She stops walking.

"Oh, hello, Thasus!", she says. "How are you? I saw that you got the attention of some of the girls."

"What? No, I don't think so…"

Now she is smiling and looking at the floor.

"It was very impressive how you brought Europa."

I approach her and hold her hand. She raises her eyes.

"It was thanks to you that I trapped her!", I say.

"What are you saying?", she laughs. She is looking straight into my eyes.

I take her other hand.

"I used a lasso, like the ones you showed me to set up. Only bigger."

"So, in a sense, *I* caught Europa", she says, a bright smile on her thick lips.

"In a sense", I reply.

And then I kiss her.

XXV

A light beam coming from a hole in the shed's ceiling wakes me up. I am lying on the straw. Artemis is gone.

Well, I know where she lives.

Images from last night flash on my mind: Artemis' lavender smell, the taste of her lips, like truffle, the feeling of holding her waist in my hands, her black hair swinging. I smile, satisfied. The happiest man in the world.

I didn't drink that much yesterday, so there's no hangover. In fact, I feel a soothing sensation on my joints. I am neither sleepy nor fully awake. For many minutes, I just enjoy the sensation of lying on the straw. I haven't felt so good since I was ten years old.

I stretch on the floor like a cat. I consider sleeping a bit more, but I don't really feel sleepy, so I stand up and put on my tunic. Through the open door, I can see the morning light. What a nice day ahead!

When I get out of the shed, I see two soldiers waiting at the entrance of the house, holding Europa. The cow looks quite docile. So much, in fact, that the soldiers are having a hard time keeping her from falling asleep on the ground! Zeus has overdone the mandragora.

Then I hear someone shouting in the house, so I run inside. The soldiers startle, but otherwise don't try to stop me.

Next to the dining table, Zeus and the Captain are discussing heatedly. None of them sees me, both of them lost in the quarrel.

Hermes hides his face in Leto's apron, near the oven. Behind her father, Artemis looks at me with a worried expression.

"I already paid you! What else do you want?"

"The taxes have gone up!", says the Captain. "The Lord wishes to own an elephant. He'll bring it all the way from India! That will require an extra effort from the good people of Nephele, but it is all for the greater good."

"But I don't have anything else! I already gave you all!"

"Not all", he says, approaching Artemis. He takes her hand; Artemis steps back. Zeus looks pained.

Me, I glance at the floor. There I meet the Harpy's eyes.

He's messing with *her* because he knows that you won't raise a finger.

"Hey!", I say.

The Captain turns around.

"What's this clown doing here?", he complains. Then he looks at Artemis. "Ah! I see. He lives here, doesn't he?"

He gets close to me.

"Sweet Artemis, since when do you fancy homosexual boys?"

Everyone is uncomfortable. The Harpy now perches on the Captain's shoulder.

You're just a coward, Thessalus, your father knew it well. If you weren't always so afraid, you would punch this asshole's mouth until he spat out his soul. But you can't, because you're a pussy. You're the most pathetic...

The Captain grabs my cheek.

"Look at him! He can't wait to suck my balls! You can't, can you?"

... so much pity for you. A seven year old! A seven year old could beat the crap out of...

I look at Artemis. She is shaking her head.

The Captain turns to her.

"Ah, Artemis! You broke my heart!"

The Captain stops. He's noticed Diana lying on the corner of the room. "But what do we have here?"

The Captain picks up the sword and examines it.

The Harpy hovers before me.

... and now he'll take it. And all you'll do is look at him like a frog, while this motherfucker steals the only thing that's left from your late father. You're not a man, you're a shame. You're the little mouse that...

"What a beautiful weapon! I bet that one can sell it in Trachis for a good price." He addresses Zeus. "You cunning peasant! Were you hiding this wonder from us?"

"It is not mine to give. It's the boy's", Zeus says, pointing at me.

"This idiot has been living in the Lord's land for a while", the Captain sentences. "Thus he must pay his taxes, like everyone else. The sword is coming with us."

...doing it! You'll let him leave with your father's sword! You sad, weak man, you pathetic wimp! You coward! You weasel!

The Captain walks by me, carrying Diana away, while the Harpy flutters next to my ear, shouting:

Coward! Weasel! Coward! Weasel! Coward! Weasel! Coward! Weasel!

Before he reaches the door, I grasp the Captain's arm.

"You're not leaving with that sword", I say.

The Captain tries to beat me with Diana's handle. He's slow: I block his attack with my left hand and punch him in the face with the right hand. The Captain drops Diana and falls on the floor.

The Captain touches his nose. He can't believe the blood on his hand.

Slowly, I pick up my sword.

"This sword stays with me", I say. "And you and that scum out there are leaving this farm right now!" The words have come out easily, I didn't need to think them.

The Captain stands up. Before he can draw his sword, I kick him on the head. My blow catapults him out of the house, he rolls over the doorsteps.

His two men are waiting outside, ten meters away from the house. They have drawn their swords. The Captain stands up and backs up a few steps to seek refuge between the two soldiers. I keep walking until I am at two meters' distance. A thought crosses my mind: "don't let them surround you".

"Kill him! Kill that son of a bitch!", shouts the Captain.

For some seconds, no one moves.

Then, the soldier on my left attempts a thrust at my stomach. I dodge the blow and cut his hand. He shouts like a pig. Meanwhile, the right guard is attempting to slash me from behind. I block his blow over my head, and quickly turn around, just in time to stop his second blow to my face. I dodge two more blows, one from either side. The second blow leaves his upper body unprotected: he's made a mistake. Extending my arm, I puncture his throat. He brings his hand to his neck, but it's too late.

There's a noise behind me. The handless soldier is attacking me with a dagger. With my left forearm, I block his wrist: the knife stops at two centimeters from my nose. I get close to him, and so does my blade. My sword enters cleanly just below his sternum and pricks his heart.

I turn around before his body meets the ground. Where is the Captain? I can see him, running towards the house. In the door's threshold, Artemis, Leto and Zeus look at the scene, horrified. Hermes stands numb in front of his mother. The Captain is about to reach them…

Suddenly, my sword is no longer in my hand: it is spinning towards the Captain. It strikes him when he reaches the doorsteps.

The tip of the sword is thrust in the Captain's back. He's lying in front of the entrance.

I get close and take the sword out. The Captain screams. I put him on his back.

"You are all dead!", he shouts. "I will get you hanged!"

"No, you won't", I say, piercing his heart.

He is still looking at me, surprised of being dead. I kneel beside him and close his eyes. I breathe deeply. On my right I can hear Europa peacefully snoring on the ground. Everything is quiet again.

Looking up, I see Zeus and his family still on the threshold. Zeus and Leto are looking at me in a strange manner. Artemis is giving me her back, she's crying. Zeus says:

"Oh, Thasus! Oh, oh, Thasus! What have you done?"

I walk to the house, but Leto shrieks and takes Hermes inside. They're scared of me! Artemis turns around. She's looking at me with disappointment.

"What is the matter, Zeus? Are you scared? Don't be! While I'm here, no one will dare touching you or your family." I bump my chest with my sword's handle. "Let the Lord send more men, let them all come! I will kill them! I will kill them all!"

Zeus addresses Artemis:

"He can't stay here: they'll hang him." He gets close to the Captain and turns him around. He takes his money bag. He hands it to me.

"There you are, Thasus", he says. "Take this; you'll need it." To Artemis: "bring him to the northern road and come back immediately. No one can see you, understood?"

Artemis gestures towards the bodies: "what will you do with them?"

Zeus points at the fields. Artemis nods and enters the house hastily.

"Zeus!", I say. "Let me stay! I'll protect you and your family, I swear!"

"Listen to me, Thasus", he says, looking into my eyes. "This is not safe for my family. You need to leave my land now."

"But I ..."

Artemis is holding my arm. She hands me my sheath and my bag of utensils. Without a word, we leave the farm.

Artemis is walking very fast. At the beginning, I think that she's taking me to the city, but soon we take a detour through a small fir forest.

"Where are we going?", I ask.

"I'm taking you to a big road that heads north."

We walk for some more time.

"Artemis, I had to do something."

She doesn't reply.

"He harassed your father! In front of all your family!"

"Be careful with these bushes", she says.

Silence.

"He addressed you in such a disgusting way..."

She stops. She points at a lane at the end of the forest. I feel that she's about to cry. When she talks, she looks at the ground.

"That is the road to the north. It leads to Melitaea: there you can ask for directions. Take this." She hands me her bow and her quiver, all the while looking at the ground.

"Artemis, did you hear what that monster did to Homer in the bar? He threatened to tear off his eyes!"

Suddenly, Artemis stares at me in the eye.

"Stop it", she says. "You didn't slaughter these men to protect me, my family or Homer. You killed them for the same reason you killed the leopard: because you can't stand not being the hero."

"That's not true! I wanted to protect…!"

"What you did will haunt my family! The Lord will not rest until he finds out what became of his men. Everyone's in danger because you wanted to look brave!"

I explode.

"They're in danger because they're cowards! How many men has the Lord? Twenty, thirty? There must be like a hundred men in Nephele: why don't they fight back? Aren't they tired of being bullied? When is enough?"

"They are not cowards! They are men and women who work the land hard: their families need them to survive another winter. They don't go to war because they fear for their children and they are not trying to impress anybody. Don't you have any compassion?"

"Compassion? I don't have compassion for wimps!", I shout. "Cowardice kills good men! If they're too scared to fight for their lives, then they're better off dead. I wouldn't have a single brave warrior sacrifice himself to defend those pathetic little shits!"

Artemis looks at me, incredulous. She gives a few steps back and then runs off.

I walk up to the road and stand there grumbling for a while.

I think of returning to the farm, but, in the end, I take out my map and try to orient myself. I have a long way ahead.

XXVI

The god Ares never forgave my father for the death of his daughter Hecate, the sea monster of Seriphos. His heart crying for vengeance, Ares traveled to the North East and made a pact with the barbarian Scynthians. These nomadic people followed Ares from the Arabian peninsula through Thrace, devastating every city, town or village they found in their way.

Soon, news of their wicked ways reached my father's court. The barbarians had burned Ainos to the ground. The barbarians had cut the right hand of every man in Abdera. In Eion, they had killed all adults and left the children in charge. In Aena, the Scynthians had thrown tons of salt in the river that fed the fields, making them barren.

My father was the first to guess Ares' plan. In the next few months, the Scynthians would reach Macedonia. And then Thessaly, and Aetolia, and Doris and Locris. They would destroy everything. It would be the end of civilization.

Without a day to spare, my father traveled to Trachis, Delphi, Thebes, Athens. He spoke in front of councils, assemblies and kings. As a result of his efforts, a large alliance of poleis against the Eastern invaders was founded: the Ionian League.

Ionian League troops, commanded by my father, stopped the Scynthians from taking Tricca, in Thessaly. That was the first defeat of the barbarians, who escaped West, to the Pindus mountain, to recover.

Ares took the chance to forge alliances with the communities inhabiting Thesprotia. Despite the fact that Thesprotians spoke a dialect of Greek, the Greeks from the south regarded them as semi-barbaric: they refused to commerce with them or let them live in their poleis. Most

Thesprotian kingdoms welcomed the chance to fight the arrogant southerners.

So the Northern Axis was established.

The Northern Axis defeated the Ionian League in Phthiotis and Doris. However, they were unable to penetrate Aetolia, and thus reach Pleuron. My father's army repelled them every single time. Since the war hadn't interrupted sea commerce, the Ionian League could keep receiving supplies from the south almost indefinitely. The Northern Axis was in a completely different state. In order to avoid an attack from the rear-guard, they had systematically devastated all the cities they encountered on their way south. They had counted on pillaging more cities as they advanced. When the Ionian League stopped them, the army of the Northern Axis started running out of supplies.

Then Ares made his move.

One of the communities joining the Northern Axis was Ephira, the city-state of the centaur Chiron, my father's master. Leaving his army stationed in Doris, Ares visited the king of Ephira and convinced him to send Chiron to the battlefield. Being a general of the Ephira army, Chiron couldn't refuse a direct order from the king. He said goodbye to his wife and sons and left for Doris.

The soldiers of the Ionian League were restless. So far, they had felt very confident fighting along the great Thasus, the almighty warrior with the winged golden helmet who rode a pegasus.

In the last days, however, they had heard some disturbing rumors. Apparently, a monster had recently joined the Scynthian troops. He was part animal, part human: strong as a beast, clever like a philosopher. The monster was old, very old. In fact, some of the oldest soldiers had encountered him in the past. They told stories of fire and blood, of whole armies slaughtered in the course of a night. They recounted how the monster had extinguished the sun and dried the sea.

That's why, when a three-meters tall black centaur entered the Ionian camp one evening, no one dared to stop him.

Chiron didn't ask anybody for directions: he found my father's tent by the smell.

"Thasus! Get out!", he thundered.

When my father came out of his tent and saw Chiron, he felt very happy. And he hugged the centaur, and the centaur hugged him back, and they both cried, for they hadn't seen each other for two decades.

My father hosted Chiron in his tent. Candles were lit, and wine and lamb were relished, while my father and Chiron recalled the old times.

At one point of the night, the spirit of wine left the two warriors. Chiron said, his voice broken:

"You and I are fighting tomorrow."

"I know", replied my father. "But I don't understand why. These Scythians can't but bring chaos to our world. Why is Ephyra supporting them?"

"The king fears that, should he not help them, they will raid the kingdom."

"That won't happen: we won't let them!", said my father. "Ephyra is welcome to join the Ionian League..."

"Thasus, it's pointless", interrupted Chiron. "Our king is weak. Even worse: he is an idiot, and Ares is playing him like a lyre. But he is my king, and I will fight to death if he orders me to."

Chiron stood up and trotted out of the tent. My father followed. The two warriors hugged and Chiron left.

The next morning, my father descended from the skies sitting on Boreas. Chiron was already waiting in the battlefield. They got close and hugged. Behind each warrior, there was an army.

"So, are we doing this?", asked my father.

Chiron nodded.

"This is not right."

Chiron attacked first, thrusting his sword straight at my father's heart. He failed: my father blocked the blow with his shield. Then the armies behind the two men ran towards each other. The battle of Evenus had started.

Soldiers from one and another side fought bravely to slash each other's throats. Meanwhile, Chiron was busy trying to kill his former student.

Decades ago, Chiron had defeated a young Thasus without much effort. This time, though, he found himself to be no match for the powerful warrior that my father had become. My father blocked blow after blow, until Chiron's sword broke.

"It is over, Chiron", said my father, tending his hand. "I implore you! Let's leave the battlefield together!"

In response, Chiron took out a dagger and sprang onto my father. Both warriors rolled over, desperately trying to cut and not be cut. Soon, the fight was over. Chiron was lying on a pool of blood. My father, panting, was standing close to him. He had a stab wound on his side and he was crying.

His master was dead.

My father lost it. He started shouting Ares' name. He cursed him and threatened the god. He called him names, he dared him to come meet him in the battlefield.

And the god Ares came. He came walking from the north, a silver helmet on his hand and a sword on his waist. He had a black beard and wicked gleaming dark eyes. Everyone stopped fighting and made him room. No one talked, they hardly dared to breathe.

Ares came close to my father. He smiled and whispered:

"It's been centuries since the last time I was in the battlefield. You have convinced me to return. Congratulations."

"Oh, shut up!", said my father, punching the god on the mouth.

Ares was thrown several meters away. He stood up almost immediately. Without a word, he put on his helmet and, grabbing his sword, he jumped into the skies.

He landed just in front of my father. He threw my father a strong uppercut, that sent him high up and down to the hard ground.

My father stood up and spat some blood. Then, without warning, he sprinted towards the god. Ares raised his arms to protect himself, but my father's punch made him roll anyway.

Ares was still rolling when my father grabbed one of his legs and threw him away as if he were a ragged doll. Ares landed on the floor badly, but he had the time to draw his sword before my father reached him. Still running, my father drew his sword.

The two warriors crossed their swords. And, every time their weapons clashed, it was like a thunderclap. And the birds flew away, and the skies turned black, and the soil below the fighters' feet broke into pieces.

My father had never been so angry. He kept throwing blows at the god who had sent his mentor to death.

Ares couldn't keep the pace: his sword flew in the air. And my father made his first blood, slashing the god's chest. Ares fell on the ground and my father sank his sword on his heart.

The god cried in pain, but still lived. When my father cut both of Ares' arms, a new pair started growing from the wounds. Blind with fury, my father tossed away his sword and jumped onto Ares' body. He punched his face until Ares' skull cracked. He lifted Ares on his arms and broke *the god's back with his knee. Sitting on the god's chest, he kept punching, kicking and twisting the evil god.*

Some time, perhaps hours later, all of Ares' bones were broken. The god was screaming for mercy, blood flowing from his six orifices. And yet he wouldn't die.

Someone tapped my father's shoulder; it was the goddess Athena.

"Thasus, stop", she said. "It won't work."

My father left Ares and turned towards the goddess.

"He made me kill Chiron!", he cried, hugging Athena's waist.

"I know", replied Athena, caressing my father's head. "That's the way my brother is. That's what he's always done."

"He will do it again and again. He won't stop until we men are all dead. He won't stop until the whole world is a ball of flames!"

Athena looked at my father gravely, tears running down her cheeks. She said:

"No, Thasus. I won't let him. I won't let any of them harm you again. From now on, no god, giant or Titan will ever mess with your kind. I will make sure, I swear."

That said, Athena picked her brother's agonizing body and left the battlefield.

Soon, the surviving soldiers also abandoned the scene: nobody wanted to fight any more. Scynthians and Thesprotians departed to the north; the rest returned to their homes in the south. Only one figure remained in the battlefield.

My father, the great Thasus, was left alone.

XXVII

I walk for several days. After my morning exercises, I eat *horta* and hunt hares and small birds. I try to avoid cities and villages: I sleep far from the main road, looking at the stars, my leopard skin over my body. The weather's getting cold, so I buy a woolen tunic from a merchant I meet on the road. Some days I think of Artemis, and my heart feels heavy. Those days I walk faster; I focus on the cold air cooling my head.

On my fourth day, I reach the foothills of mount Olympus. Bringing the pendant to my forehead, I whisper:

"My dear Priestess, I did it. I arrived at the house of the gods."

Save a couple of oaks and laurel trees, the mountain is all rocks and lichen. I see no paths, so I just start walking up the slope.

Soon I am crossing a forest of beech and black pine trees. The trees hide the sun completely: it feels like walking under bed sheets. The ground is dark brown, there are barks and trunks covered with moss. I take off my sandals to feel the soft soil under my feet. Everything is so quiet.

Some kilometers ahead, I see a lion resting a few meters to my left. He blends well within the vegetation; that's why I didn't see him before. He's also noticed me. He stands on his fours and turns into my direction.

I stop and turn towards him. We look at each other for a while. Finally, he turns away and leaves. He has realized that I am not scared and doesn't want to find the reason.

The forest leads to a meadow full of bright green grass. There is a very strong and cold wind coming from the north. I see a few pine trees around, but all the branches are pointing to the south. Seen from the side, they look funny, as if some giant had cut off half of the tree.

As I climb, a white mist starts covering it all. Soon, I can hardly see my own feet. I shouldn't keep walking. I could fall through a cliff, or stumble on a rock. But it's too cold: I can't just camp either. I keep walking very slowly and with great care, looking for a cave or a large rock; anything that can stop the damned winds which are driving me mad.

When I can hardly walk anymore, I see a yellow light in front of me. A bonfire? I hurry up. I can't feel my toes anymore.

Soon I'm facing a house made of clay. The yellow light is coming from a small window in the facade. I desperately bang the black wooden door.

A very old woman opens it. She is very short and wears a thick black dress. Her thin face is full of wrinkles.

"You again?", she asks. I don't understand what she means.

"I'm freezing!", I say.

She looks around, annoyed.

"Come in."

The house has wooden floors. The entrance leads to a kitchen, where a golden oven burns pine wood. It is heating a small pot. To the right, I see a large table with many chairs.

I just stand in front of the oven until the old woman offers me a chair. I am shivering.

"I was about to eat", she says. "Do you want some hot soup?"

I nod. Soon we are both sitting at opposite sides of the table. The soup has chickpeas and boar, I wonder where she got them from. It tastes very good. Soon I feel my toes again. But I feel so tired...!

"What was your name?"

"Thessalus", I reply.

"Ah, yes, Thessalus. Yes, I remember."

Did she? Did I ever tell her my name?

"What is your name?", I ask.

She answers. As soon as she says her name, I have forgotten it.

I look around.

"This is a very big house. Do you live alone?"

Her tired eyes inspect the long table.

"I used to live with my sisters. Now it's just me."

"What did you and your sisters do?"

She thinks for a moment.

"Lots of people came and went, but where were they headed? That I can't remember, it was a long time ago. Anyway, hardly anyone comes here anymore".

"How long have you been alone?"

She considers the question. Then she explodes:

"I don't know! What is wrong with you? Why are you asking so many questions?"

She is very agitated. I stand up and hold her hands.

"I'm sorry, madam, I'm such an impolite guest. By the way, thanks for the soup! It was delicious."

"The soup? What soup?"

I point at the pot.

"Ah, yes. You're welcome."

She waves me away and paces around the room for a while. She's trying to come up with something to do, whatever, anything that makes sense.

"Let me take you to your bed", she concludes.

She lights an old oil lamp and I follow her through a long corridor, with doors on each side every few meters. The house must have been an inn of some sort.

We stop at a door at the end.

"This is our largest room. I trust that you'll be comfortable here."

She hands me the lamp and runs back to the dining room. She is surprisingly fast.

The room is in very good condition. There is a large wooden bed with a straw mattress, a small desk and a chair. A crown of mint leaves hangs on the wall. Everything is very clean.

I strip and slide inside the blankets. I stretch my legs and arms. The bed feels very comfortable. I blow off the lamp and fall asleep almost immediately.

XXVIII

When I wake up, I find that the lady has just prepared breakfast: eggs, ham and *horta*. They are on a large tray on the wooden table, the eggs still steaming.

"Come take a seat. I have the impression that you like greasy stuff!", she says, smiling.

"I do!", I reply. "Thanks for this banquet, everything looks delicious!"

"Oh, you're such a dear!"

"Could I ask you…? I think that yesterday I didn't get your name."

She says her name, clearly and slowly. This time I repeat it to myself over and over, to memorize it.

"Please, start without me. I need to find something", she says, and disappears in the long corridor.

#

I have finished breakfast, but the lady hasn't returned yet. I open the main door and pace for some minutes outside the house. It's no longer cold and windy, but the mist is still there. There's no way I'm leaving today.

I return to the house and start looking for the woman. I don't find her anywhere in the ground floor, so I take the stairs leading to the first floor.

I find myself in another long corridor. Despite the thin rectangular windows close to the end of the stairs, most of the corridor is in darkness. One of the side doors at the end of the hallway is open, though: a milky light illuminates the entrance. As I approach the room, I hear the lady talking to herself.

The room is full of wooden trunks. The lady kneels on the floor, inspecting the contents of one of them. Around her lie papyri, lenses, mirrors, statuettes and candles of various shapes.

"I finished breakfast."

"Ah!". She looks at me. "Do you want lunch?"

"Not yet, thanks. Can I accompany you?"

"Sure!", she says, tapping the floor beside her.

I move some junk away and sit down.

"Getting rid of old stuff?", I ask.

"No", she replies, resuming her inspection of the trunk. "I'm trying to find something."

"Can I help you? What are you looking for?".

"I'm not sure. I'll tell you when I see it." She stares at an iron key for a while, then discards it.

For some minutes, the lady keeps taking stuff from the trunk and tossing it on the floor.

"Yesterday you said that you knew me", I say, to break the silence. "However, this is my first time here, and I don't think we've met before."

She stops.

"Nonsense. You were here some time ago, I remember it very clearly."

"When?"

She thinks hard before answering.

"I don't remember when", she finally says.

"What was I doing here?"

"You came looking for someone. A man."

"Did I find him?"

"I guess...", she says. Suddenly, she brings her hand to her mouth. "When you came back, you buried *something* in the yard."

"What did I bury?"

"That I didn't see."

I look at her with expectation. She continues:

"The stone behind the house. You lifted it as if it were made of feathers! Then you placed something below and left the stone where it was."

I excuse myself and hurry downstairs.

#

The stone is white and has the shape of a round omelet. It is twenty centimeters thick, with a diameter of about two meters. There are no other rocks around: perhaps this one used to be a sundial. It is covered in moss.

Sticking my fingers under it, I try to lift it. It doesn't move.

I catch my breath. Second try.

My feet are sunk into the ground. I can feel my head getting red. I pull and pull, I curse and blow, but the damned thing doesn't move an inch.

While I recover, I amble around the rock, taking deep breaths. The morning air is very clean. The mist is thick, though: from where I am, I can hardly see the house.

Then I discover something.

On the surface of the stone, half-hidden by moss, I can read the letter "Θ": something is carved on the edge of the rock. I squat and tear the moss apart.

Now I am standing back, looking at the inscription. It says "Θεσσαλός". Thessalus.

Back on the road, what did the Priestess say? It was something like: "to find your father, you must find yourself". Did she mean this? Will I find my dead father below this stone?

I must do it. I must lift the stone.

I place my fingers just below my name. They stick to the bottom of the rock. I feel a shiver down my spine. My feet are well planted on the ground, as if they were part of the soil. Everything is quiet, everything fits in place.

I pull. I pull with all my strength. My forearms, my fingers, everything hurts. I start feeling dizzy. I am shouting something, but I cannot understand what.

And then, the rock moves. First it's just a millimeter, then a handspan. All of a sudden, the rock is at my waist. Nothing hurts anymore. I'm doing it! I am lifting the rock!

Then I see the bundle. It is right in front of my feet, a little grey sack. I kick it away and let the stone fall back on the ground. It makes a deafening sound.

My hands feel funny, the skin on the base of my fingers hard as steel. I look at the rock. I can't believe that I lifted *that*.

The bundle. It is on the floor, a piece of wool closed with a simple knot. There is something very important inside.

I squat and undo the knot. Something shines. A cuirass, a chest plate. And below, a helmet. A golden helmet with metal wings on the sides. The helmet forged by the god Hephaestus. The helmet of the man who traveled inside a giant eel, overpowered the snake of Megara and defeated the god of war.

One summer evening, many years ago, I asked my father about this helmet. I remember it very vividly. I am a little boy. My father and my mother are sitting outside our house, holding hands. The sun is about to set. It is hot and humid.

"What helmet?", asks my father.

"Your winged helmet, Bampás! You are wearing one in the relief at the council house of Eleusis. And in all your statuettes, and in the pictures of an amphora, and, and…".

"Ah! That helmet!", he says.

He looks at the sky, a smile on his face.

"I left it somewhere."

"You lost it?", I burst. "You lost the helmet of Hephaestus!?"

"Thessalus! Look!", interrupts my mother.

The sun is setting. It is so red! My father holds me under his left arm. With his right arm he hugs my mother. No one says anything for a while.

When the sky has turned green, I free myself from my father's embrace and announce:

"Bampás! When I grow up, I'll be stronger than you. And I'll wear your golden helmet and your steel armor. And I will fight barbarians. And I will live adventures and marry a princess in a faraway land."

My father chuckles, his laughter deep like thunder. "I bet you will, son, I bet you will!"

I think about that moment, one of the best of my life.

#

I want to show the lady what I found, but I can't find her anywhere in the house. She's neither in the living room nor on the second floor. And I can't call her: once more, I have forgotten her name.

Frustrated, I check one by one all the rooms in the ground floor. The house is big, with many corridors I haven't noticed before. It is all very confusing: more than once I have problems to find my way back to the kitchen. At times, I have the impression that I am walking the same path over and over.

At last, I find the lady in a sort of storage room. She's sitting on the floor, manipulating a small metallic object.

"I can't!", she complains. "I've tried hard, but it just won't open!"

She hands me the piece. It is a bronze cubic box, about twenty centimeters wide. The metal is almost completely green, it must be very old. On the top it has a narrow slot.

I stick my nail in the slot and pull, but the lid doesn't move: something is keeping it locked. I try to pry the box open, but the box is perfectly smooth and a bit too large for my hand. I just can't get hold of the lid.

"What's inside?", I ask the lady.

She looks at me with wide eyes. "You don't remember?"

"No", I say, "I don't."

But somehow, I do. I see myself somewhere, a long time ago, opening this box and taking something out. It is something vague, with no shape or color. It has a name, but one can't say it aloud.

Frustrated, I turn to the slot on the box. Where did I see it before?

Of course! In the Agora, in Athens. There was this machine that served water in exchange for a coin. It had a narrow, rectangular slot, just like this one.

I take off my pendant. The Priestess gave me that pendant less than a year ago, but it feels like I had worn it all my life. I untie the old coin and, for the last time, look at the engraved woman with the helmet and the spear.

Goodbye, my good friend.

I slide the coin into the slot. It fits perfectly. The box shakes as if something were moving inside. I hear a click, and suddenly the lid is loose.

I open the box and peek inside.

XXIX

I am climbing the Mythikas peak. It is cold, but there is no wind. There is no mist, or any clouds, for that matter. The sun's shinning over my head.

But something is wrong. I don't quite remember how I ended up here.

I remember opening the lady's box and taking out what was inside. Strangely, I recall the scene from the outside. That is, I can see myself holding something in my hands. But my back is turned towards me, so I can't see what it is that I'm holding.

Anyway, the lady is very happy. In fact, we are both laughing. She doesn't look that old in my memory. Her hair is black and most of her wrinkles are gone. Now she looks around 30. She says something, but I can't hear it. I can't hear anything. She accompanies me to the living room.

Then I guess that I went out and saw that the mist was gone. I must have returned to my room to pick up my things, I must have said the lady goodbye. And then I must have walked for some hours.

But I don't remember any of that. I was climbing up the mountain and then I realized that some memories were missing.

I stop walking and look back. There's no sign of the lady's house.

#

I find the palace in the afternoon, lying at the end of a large plateau. There are other constructions scattered around, but the palace is the only one still standing. It looks like an old temple, only much larger. It has three steps, the crepidoma, over which about twenty Doric columns rest, supporting an architrave, a frieze, and a golden triangular roof, the tympanon. The frieze is decorated with red and blue geometrical figures. There are no sculptures at all, the tympanon completely void. Behind the palace, the Mythikas peak rises.

I am not alone: there are wild black horses trotting around. I don't understand what they're doing here, in this barren land, when they could be happily grazing some kilometers down the mountain. They look strong and healthy, though. The horses do not disturb me while I walk towards the palace. The palace.

I find him in a palace. My father and I stare at each other, and then my quest is over.

Climbing up the crepidoma, I walk through the columns and enter the naos. It is empty and is surprisingly narrow, just about ten meters wide. There are six rows of doors on each side.

I enter the second one on my right, and I find myself in what looks like a bedroom. There's a small window and a wooden bed. The bed is undone: half of the blanket is lying on the floor. In fact, the bedroom is in a very poor state. There's no dust around, but there are several objects on the floor: a string musical instrument built over the shell of a tortoise, some papers with diagrams and a strange metallic construction. I approach the bed and touch the mattress. It's cold.

I search the other rooms. In one I find colored seashells, a net and a large pile of salt. Another one is decorated with crowns of red roses, a large silver mirror and perfumed candles. Another one has a broken armor and drops of blood. One gets the impression that the rooms were occupied just a few seconds before.

I keep walking through the naos until I face a second door: the palace has an *adyton*. I cross the door and find myself in a large room with white walls. Sunlight coming from long, thin windows fills the room. In the distance I can see a large rectangular table, with many chairs around.

As I approach the table, I count twelve seats. The table is set: there's a plate in front of each chair. And wine bowls, and forks, and many jars.

But the jugs are empty. And so are the plates and the bowls.

"They're not here", a voice says behind me.

Startled, I turn around and see an old man dressed in skins. His grey hair, long and dirty, falls in disarray over his shoulders. A thick beard covers half of his face. Hanging from his belt there's a small leather bag, a long knife… and a beautiful lyre.

"I have been waiting for so long…"

XXX

When the battle of Evenus concluded, my father didn't return to Pleuron. Instead, he wandered for many years in the wild.

He avoided all human contact. He would sleep in caves or on trees, far away from any town or road: he was done with mankind. In time, his clothes turned into tatters and he started wearing animal skins to protect himself from the cold night. A desperate man, he wouldn't stay for long in the same place, always traveling, always walking forward. He hardly slept: the vision of his master Chiron dying at his hands was always there to haunt him.

One day, while lying on a grass field, my father heard a woman scream. My father stood up and saw a young girl running from a giant brown bear. Not noticing my father, the girl passed just a few meters from him. The bear, some meters behind, hadn't seen my father yet.

My father hadn't met a person in years. He had come to think that he felt nothing for his fellow men. However, the girl's calls for help awakened something in him, something that had been asleep for a long, long time.

Sprinting towards the bear, my father pushed him with all his might. The bear rolled over several meters away, then stood up. He was at least five meters tall. Staring at my father, he roared viciously.

My father was not intimidated. Decisive, he walked towards the bear. And man and beast looked into each other's eyes.

The bear attacked with a swipe. Dodging the bear's claws, my father punched him on the stomach. The bear backed up some meters, but didn't fall: his back claws were sunk on the ground.

The bear then fell over my father, and the two rolled over, with my father punching and kicking the beast with his knees and the bear striking my father with arms thick like trees. The fight did not last long: my father managed to grab the bear's neck from behind and, using his legs and arms, broke the monster's spine.

My father had won the fight, but he was wounded: his right arm was bleeding from the bear's swipes. He sat on the floor and, using a stone, cut a piece of skin from the bear. He tried to bandage his arm with the skin, but he wasn't able to tie it.

The girl, who had seen the combat from the distance, kneeled beside my father and tied the bandage. My father stirred but didn't protest. It was the first time in years that someone had laid hands on him.

He looked up and contemplated the youth. She had a short curly black hair, big brown eyes, thick lips and a small nose. She was very short. My father contemplated her delicate hands while she was securing the bandage to his arm. Her dress didn't fully cover her shoulders, dark and smooth. She smelled of truffles.

Abruptly, the girl lifted her glance and smiled. And suddenly my father couldn't breathe. It wasn't just her white teeth or sensual lips, but that innocent, happy expression. The sweetest smile in the whole world!

The girl took my father to a nearby village, Tyria, where she and her parents managed a small farm. Soon the girl's family would offer him food and shelter for the night, and a doctor would come to tend his wounds. However, while my father was walking towards what would become his new home, he could only think of how good it felt holding hands with that sweet farm girl.

The girl was my mother, of course. Some months later, she and my father married. With the help of some villagers, my father built a small farm near the land of his in-laws. I was born shortly after.

My mother and my father cultivated melons, apples, oranges and olives. From time to time, my father went out hunting and returned with a boar over his shoulders. Or a rabbit, or a gazelle, or a lion. In the evenings, my family would sit on the fields to watch the sunset. My mother would drink an herb infusion and enjoy the fresh air and the chirp of the crickets. My father would sit me on his lap and tell me stories of his youth. He would speak of kings, monsters and gods. He would tell me how he was gobbled by a giant eel, and how he once caught a winged horse.

My father couldn't wait to train me in the art of war. He taught me how to wrestle, how to shoot with bow and arrow, the use of the spear and the sword. With ten years old, I was the strongest and fastest kid in Tyria. My father was so proud!

One day, when I was 17, my father and I went hunting. I loved hunting with my father! We would chat, we would play strength games. We would make a fire and roast a hare. Sometimes, when it became too dark to return home, we would lie next to each other and sleep looking at the stars. That day we were planning a short trip to a nearby lake. We would hunt some ducks and return home in a few hours.

We were not far from Tyria when a group of six men approached us in the road. They were coming from all directions. They carried daggers and swords.

My father handed me his sword and whispered: "try to break the circle. Don't let them surround you!". Then he threw himself at one of the men.

In a few seconds, my father had broken the man's neck and taken his dagger. The rest of the men ignored me and walked towards my father. One of them, who hurried too much, had his throat slashed.

The remaining four men were cleverer. None of them played hero. Instead, they approached my father at the same speed.

My father ran towards one to break the circle. He killed him, but, by then, the other three had formed a circle around him.

"Thessalus!", my father shouted. "Help me!"

I was frozen to the spot. I wanted to go there and help my father, but I had never been in combat. I was terrified. In the eye of my mind, I could see the bandit's swords piercing my head like a melon.

My father blocked a few blows, but he couldn't possibly control all the angles. It was a matter of time before the men wounded him. Desperate, he charged towards one of them. The bandit blocked the attack, but fell on the floor. Meanwhile, another bandit sank his sword on my father's back.

My father screamed.

"Thessalus!"

But I was looking at the floor, trying to become invisible.

My father kicked the leg of the fallen man, breaking it to the bone. The man cried.

Meanwhile, the assailant advanced again towards my father. This time, my father blocked his attack and countered with a thrust to the man's belly.

But he couldn't take the blade out fast enough. With a quick move, the last standing bandit sank his sword right on the center of my father's chest. My father fell to the floor. I knew that he wouldn't stand up.

"Bampás!", I cried.

The bandit turned towards me. He was smiling.

For a moment, everything turned black.

And when I recovered my vision, I was no longer scared. The bandit was saying something, but I couldn't hear him. I just heard a voice coming from my stomach. A deep, dark voice that shouted: "Kill, kill, kill!"

I walked towards the man like a bull. He threw a thrust, that I blocked with my father's sword. He backed up, throwing two more blows to stop my advance. Before he could throw a fourth blow, I hit his hand. His sword fell on the floor: my blow had slashed his four fingers.

The man was looking at his hand, incredulous, but I kept advancing. He screamed: "no!"

And my blade went through his guts. And then his lungs, and then his genitalia. And soon the man was not shouting anymore.

I looked at my father's body. The bandit with the broken leg had managed to stand on one leg, he was trying to flee.

I threw away my sword and jumped over him. We both fell. He went for my eyes, but I punched his face hard, knocking him out. I kept punching his head, though, I don't know for how long. At some point I was punching the ground, the bandit's skull broken into little pieces. I was crying:

"Bampás! Bampás!"

A strange black bird landed next to me. At first, I thought it was a crow, but then I noticed the woman's head. The tiny face was staring at me, her eyes stern.

She said:

I saw it all.

XXXI

Since I left mount Olympus more than a year ago, I have been wandering aimlessly. I travel from village to village, trading for food and shelter the skins of the animals I hunt during the day. When some friendly host or a local peasant tries to engage me in a conversation, I ignore him. I want to be left alone. I never stay more than two nights in the same place.

But today it's different. The road I took has taken me to Nephele, of all places! I want to keep walking, find somewhere else to spend the night. I don't want to see any of those warm, welcoming people. But it's dark and cold, and I'm tired and hungry. When I see the lights of the tavern, I walk towards them.

The tavern looks pretty much the same as I remember. The same paintings, the same tables, the same people. But something's different, too. The paint on the wall is cracking, the tables look a tiny bit more decrepit.

The people look definitely worse. A few are chatting softly with each other, but most of them just contemplate their drinks in silence. I recognize some faces; they all look thinner and paler.

Someone stumbles upon me. It's Homer. He is much taller, on his way to become a man.

"Sorry, Sir!"

"No worries", I reply. "I'd like to sit alone, please."

"That voice... Thasus!?"

"Hi, Homer."

"Gods! I can't believe it!"

Homer is very excited. He approaches a table, where a man and his six-year-old son have bread and beer. He grabs the kid's shoulder.

"Aion, look there!", he says, pointing in my direction. "It's Thasus!"

"Thasus, the hero?", asks the boy.

"The one!", says Homer.

The boy stands up and approaches me.

"Homer said that a year ago you killed a lion the size of a mountain."

"Homer might have exaggerated the facts", I reply.

"He's so modest!", intervenes Homer, patting my back. "Listen all! Thasus is back in town!"

"Heavens, it's true!", exclaims one of the regulars.

Some customers abandon their drinks and come close to shake hands.

"Thasus, you look so different!", says the master carpenter.

"Thasus, you look taller", says the chicken farmer.

"Thasus, you look more like a man", says the milkmaid.

Everyone wants a piece of me tonight! But I can't take it. I say:

"Please, leave me alone. I just want to sit and drink." And, with these words, I occupy an empty table in a corner.

"What's wrong with him?", someone says.

"Give him a break!", says Homer. "We don't know where he was or what extraordinary adventures he experienced since we last saw him. Thasus is tired, that's all." Then, to me: "Thasus, do you want some soup?"

"Just wine", I say.

"Father, bring Thasus a bowl of wine!", shouts Homer.

Soon I am tasting the red wine. I don't want to lock eyes with anyone, so I just stare at my bowl. It was a bad idea to come. I'm about to stand up and leave when Homer starts telling a story.

"Let me remind you all what Thasus did the last time he came by. Have you ever been to the mountain that we call 'The Eye of Tartarus'?"

Everybody is silent.

"Do you mean the Chicken Peak?", says someone.

"Well, of course *now* we call it the Chicken Peak. But, not so long ago, it was called the Eye of Tartarus. It was a damned land, with black volcanic soil and no grass or trees around. No one, not even the crows, would dare getting close to that terrifying mountain. One of its caves was said to hold an entrance to the Hades, the underworld. The entrance was guarded by the mad giant cow Europa. A monster with red eyes, teeth sharp as swords and Sulphur breath, Europa would horn, chew and spit into Hades anyone stupid enough to climb the Eye of Tartarus."

"The Old Lord sent many armed units to kill the evil Beast. None ever returned. And so the good people of Nephele learned to avoid the place. Roads around it were built, warning signs were put in place. In the light of the bonfire, mothers would scare their children with stories of the mad cow who reigned alone in her high black peak."

"One day, a foreigner came to Nephele, to this very tavern. He was handsome, strong and confident. His name was Thasus, and he claimed to be the king of Pleuron, a small polis in the South. Thasus explained that he had heard stories of a giant cow roaming the outskirts of Nephele. He wanted to catch it and bring it to Pleuron's royal farm. His kingdom was suffering an economic crisis, and he reckoned that Europa would produce enough milk to feed all his citizens."

"A couple of soldiers in the tavern overhead his story. One of them was a captain of the Lord's army, a merciless minion and tax collector, who fed on our people's fear. When the Captain heard of Thasus' plans, he couldn't stop laughing. 'You'll die in the Eye, stranger', he said, 'or I'm not a captain of the kingdom of Nephele'. Thasus replied: 'Tomorrow I will catch and subdue the Chthonic Cow, and you'll all see it.'"

"The next morning, half of Nephele was gathering at the foot of the Eye of Tartarus. Some were curious to see what would happen, others wanted to change the stranger's mind. The Captain was also there, with a few soldiers. Approaching Thasus, he whispered in his ear: 'there's no way but up for you. I ordered my archers to shoot to kill if you return from the mountain without the cow'. Thasus just nodded and walked up the mountain."

"About an hour later, we heard strange noises, like rocks crashing to each other. The earth shook, dogs whined. Many brave men laid curled on the floor. Soon we heard an incredibly loud bellow, that started a minor avalanche of small stones. Then, silence."

"We had been waiting for three hours. The sun was high in the sky. Men were drying their foreheads, women were fanning themselves with rushes. Then, another sound, this time a rough one, growing louder every minute."

"We were all alarmed. The cow was not known to abandon the mountain, but perhaps Thasus' behavior had enraged her and she wanted to teach us a lesson. Under the Captain's orders, the archers prepared their arrows."

"And then, Telemachus, who has the best eyesight, saw something in the distance. It was like a cloud of dust, moving towards us. When the cloud was one kilometer away, Telemachus shouted: 'it's the stranger!'"

"And there it was, our hero Thasus, pulling a giant wooden wheeled platform, with a defenseless Europa tied on top. The cow, large like an elephant, was mooing and howling, but she could not break Thasus' knots."

"That night, there was a big celebration in Thasus' honor. We drank, we sang and we laughed. The next day, Thasus left for Pleuron with his monstrous cow."

"And what about the Captain? Well, after witnessing Thasus' bravery and strength, he felt so embarrassed as a warrior that he and two of his men left Nephele for good."

When Homer concludes his story, one man cries:

"Hurray for Thasus!".

And another one:

"Thasus, the great warrior!"

And the milkmaid:

"Thasus, the handsome hero!"

I don't want to feed their mood, so I focus on my drink. It is my second one, I'm starting to get tipsy.

The kid Aion tugs Homer's tunic.

"Homer, Homer, Homer! Can you please tell me the story of how Thasus was eaten by a sea monster?"

"Sure, Aion! Let's go back to your table and I'll tell you all about Thasus' three labors." And off they go.

Some time later, when I have just finished my third drink, a woman and a child enter the tavern.

It takes me some seconds to recognize them. They look so thin!

"Thasus!", shouts the child, when he sees me. He and his mother come to my table.

"Hello, Hermes", I say, giving him a tired smile. "Hello, Leto."

I don't want to talk to these two. I don't want to hear of Artemis' recent marriage, or be introduced to her new husband.

But Hermes and Leto don't speak. They just stare at me, hesitant.

"What's new?", I ask.

"You've got to help us, Thasus", says Hermes hastily. "Father and Artemis were arrested."

I look at Leto. She adds:

"Since you left, the Lord has increased the taxes twice. The whole town is starving! My husband stood against the Lord's men, and they arrested him. Artemis tried to stop them. She…" She starts crying.

"She used her bow", I finish. Leto nods.

"Now they're both in the Lord's dungeons", says Hermes. "We don't know if they're still alive!"

"When did all this happen?", I ask.

"Last week", says Hermes. "We didn't know what to do! And then, our neighbor tells us that you're back in town. When I heard it, I told mum: 'we have to see Thasus! He'll rescue Dad and Artemis!'"

Everybody is looking at us. They want me to save the day, but I'm not having any of it.

"What do you want from me?", I ask Hermes. "Your father and Artemis kicked me out of Nephele!"

"But …!"

"But what? This is not what you expected, Hermes? You thought that I'd 'kill the baddies', just because you asked me to?"

"You are so strong…"

"You're a coward!", I snap. Then I stand up and look at the people in the bar. "All of you are. For years, you've let them abuse you. And none of you ever thought of fighting back? You need some hero to do the dirty work because you're too busy crapping on your tunics?"

I turn to Hermes.

"You know what, Hermes? I'll do it. If you attack just one soldier, I'll fight to death."

I take off my sword and give it to Hermes. He doesn't want to take it, but I squeeze the hilt in his fist.

"There you are, Hermes. Now you're a warrior too! Come on, we're going to the Lord's palace."

But Hermes doesn't move.

"What's wrong, Hermes? You don't dare? You expect me to go risk my life to save your father and your sister, but you won't raise a finger? What's wrong with you, Hermes? What kind of son would let his own father die?".

Hermes drops the sword. He's crying.

I think about my father and the bandits, and how I also couldn't get myself to save him.

And all of a sudden I feel Hermes' pain burning in my chest. And I can't breathe and tears are running down my cheeks, because my poor father is dying again.

I kneel and hug Hermes. At first he starts, then he hugs me back. And we cry in each other's arms. Because our fathers are no longer there, and we feel all alone, and the world has turned dark and cold.

The people in the bar are still watching at a distance, they don't know what to do. Someone comes close; it's the bartender. Leto steps in, gestures him to let us be. She is also crying.

After quite a while, when I manage to stop sobbing, I whisper in Hermes' ear:

"Don't worry, Hermes. I'll save your father."

"And m-my sister?", he stammers.

"Yes", I chuckle. "I'll save her too."

I wipe away the tears and stand up. Everyone is staring at me.

"Listen!", I say. "This is what's going to happen."

XXXII

"Who builds a palace in a valley?", I ask myself. I am on the top of a hill, it's three in the morning, and there is no moon. Half a kilometer downhill, two soldiers guard the palace's front door. They look bored. I can see them, but they can't see me.

The master carpenter has just left. He helped me bring the carriage to this spot. He also provided the two horses. They are black like coal, and well trained: they didn't neigh a single time. They are firmly tied to each side of the carriage. Between them, the huge wheeled battery ram that the carpenter managed to assemble in just two hours.

Following the plan, I slowly count to 40 before I start the attack. I wear my father's helmet and armor. I'm scared. The odds are, I won't come out of this alive.

The Harpy alights a few meters to my left. Impatient, I confront her:

"What are you doing here? I don't have time for you."

The Harpy stares at me. Looking into her eyes, I whisper:

"Leave me alone."

At first, the Harpy hesitates. Then it takes flight and disappears into the night.

Without a sound, I spur the horses. The carriage starts moving down the hill. First slowly, then fast.

The two men at the door have heard the sound of the horses' hoofs. One of them has taken a torch. They stare clueless at the darkness.

Meanwhile, the carriage has gained a lot of speed. When it is a hundred meters from the door, I remove the bolt keeping the ram attached to the carriage and hold the horses back.

The battery ram leaves the carriage behind and crashes against the wooden door, reducing it to smithereens.

The two guards are looking at the spot where the front door used to be. When they turn back, they find me standing on the top of the carriage. I shoot two arrows: left and right. The guards fall on the floor, their foreheads pierced by my wood.

I jump off the carriage and cross the gate.

The palace looks exactly like the villagers said it would. I find myself in a large patio. To my left there is a large two-story building, the Lord's lodgings; to my right, a one-story roofed, long house, the soldiers' barracks. The battery ram has collided against a storeroom of some sort, breaking one of the walls. I can see wheat coming out of the wall hole, it's spilling on the floor. To the left of the storeroom I notice the passage to the second patio.

I keep walking.

"Keres!", I shout. "Come out of your den! I'm going to kill you!"

On my right, I see a soldier coming out of the barracks. I pierce his head with an arrow. Two more soldiers come out of the main building; my arrows kill them too.

"Keres, here I am! The man who killed your captain, the man who killed your leopard! Come out and fight me!"

Four soldiers have abandoned the barracks, protecting their bodies with leather shields. I shoot one of them on the foot. He drops his shield and I pierce his head. The other three soldiers charge with their spears. I shoot three arrows in the air. They puncture a leg, a head and a shoulder.

"Keres! You're dead!"

I move on. Another soldier comes out of the house, but I shoot him straight in the heart. I've run out of arrows, so I throw away my bow and my quiver.

In front of the passage leading to the second patio, a small group soldiers has formed an improvised phalanx. Without slowing down, I draw my sword.

The soldiers point their spears and charge. I recall my father's training: "when chased by a phalanx, run in circles." But I don't have time for that. I run straight towards them.

When I reach the man in the center, I jump over his shield and execute a somersault. While I turn in midair, the tip of my sword slashes the soldier's skull. As always, I land on my feet. Now I am behind the phalanx.

With a blow, I cut the legs of the man immediately on my right. Then I pierce the neck of the man on my left. Both men fall, the rest try to escape. The phalanx is dissolved.

I chase the man on my right and hit his back with my sword. I turn around to find another soldier attempting a thrust with his spear! I dodge the attack by rolling on the floor towards the attacker. I stab him on the stomach.

The remaining two soldiers have dropped their shields: they attempt a double attack. With a quick move, I throw my sword to the man on my right. He falls on the ground, his head broken in two.

The last soldier makes a thrust. I jump over the spear and, holding it with my hands, I do a handspring, my feet crashing against his nose.

I take my sword from the soldier's still body and look around. I have killed six men.

Suddenly, I feel a bump on the skull. Instinctively, I bring my hand to my head. There's a dent on the back of the helmet. Then I notice an arrow on the floor, just behind me. My father's helmet has saved my life.

Looking back, I find a young soldier, not older than fifteen, holding my bow. He is terrified. I wink at him. He drops the bow and runs off. Clever boy.

I enter the second patio. There are no buildings here, just the large theater surrounded by high walls. There's no one around. Nonetheless, I keep going on.

"Where are you hiding, Keres? This palace will be your grave!"

I stop when I reach the stage. When I look back, soldiers are entering the theater through the narrow passage.

The soldiers descend the theater's stairs, but do not dare entering the stage. There must be sixty of them.

Two elder soldiers, clearly captains, come down to the first row of stairs. One of them is short and thin; the other one, fat and tall. The short one asks:

"Who are you?"

I say: "My name--", and I stop short.

Yes. Of course.

"My name is Thasus of Pleuron.

Before I grew a beard, I smashed Hephestus' Automaton.

I was gobbled by the sea-monster of Seriphos.

I captured the immortal snake of Megara.

I flew over Greece on a winged horse.

I fought the god of war, made him beg for mercy.

I crippled the giant bandit of Athens.

I strangled the vicious beast of Nephele.

I abducted the Chthonic Cow in the Eye of Tartarus.

I entered the house of the gods.

I am not immortal, but I don't die either.

I am Thasus, the hero."

The fat captain hesitates. "What do you want?", he finally asks.

"Your boss. Hand him to me and leave this place for good. If you do that right now, I'll spare your lives."

"He's just a farmer!", says the thin captain. "Soldiers, ch...!" Before he finishes his sentence, I throw my sword at him. The sword pierces his heart, he dies instantaneously.

The soldiers are shouting like chicken. However, the fat captain quickly recovers.

"Soldiers, raise your weapons!", he orders. "He is unarmed and we are many. He has no chance! Do not play heroes, just do as I say."

The closest soldier is three meters away from me. There's no way I can escape. I am surrounded.

"Right step, march!"

Now the soldiers are two and a half meters away.

"Right step, march!"

The soldiers are now at two meters. All they have to do is thrust their spears...

"Right step, march!"

Before they can comply, a soldier falls on the floor. And then another one, and another one.

The whole army looks behind. Up ahead, on the highest stands of the theater, the villagers of Sephele are shooting arrows at the soldiers.

The captain looks at me, fully aware that he's fallen into a trap. It is then, watching his terrified expression, when I know that we will win this battle. They are more and better trained, but they are afraid. And we aren't.

I run to the captain. He draws his sword but he's too slow. Before he can throw a blow, I'm already in front of him, grabbing his forearm with my left hand.

"Gotcha!", I say, and I punch him on the face.

He won't stand up.

I recover my sword and join the fight.

#

When the last soldier exhales his last breath, the villagers and I return to the main patio to start the assault on the Lord's headquarters. With the battery ram, we soon break the front door. The floors of the palace are covered in marble and gold. A few guards fight us, but we soon dispose of them.

Some villagers and I dash the dungeons in the cellar. The ceilings are low, the walls are dirty. The stench is revolting. When we reach the cells, we surprise the jailer trying to lock himself up in one of them. I punch him on the back and grab his key ring.

We find Artemis and Zeus hugging each other in a corner of one of the cells. They are asleep, or perhaps unconscious. I open the door and slap their arms.

"Artemis, Zeus, wake up! We have to get you out of this place!"

Artemis opens her eyes.

"Thasus?", she mumbles. Then Zeus awakens too.

I help Artemis stand. She is very weak, can hardly keep her balance. I pass my arm around her waist and take her out of the cell. Two villagers help Zeus out.

We reach the palace's hall and get out. Outside, many villagers await, holding their bows.

"Dad!", shouts someone, and I see little Hermes running towards us. Leto follows. Now Zeus, Artemis, Leto and Hermes are hugging each other. I step back, but Leto grabs my arm and brings me close.

By now Zeus and Artemis are clearheaded. Zeus says:

"I'm so happy that this is all over!"

"No", I say. "Not yet."

#

The palace hall is white and golden. It has a large round pool with a silvered floor in the middle of the room. On my right, a number of villagers stand undecisive in front on a marble staircase.

"Are the Lord's chambers up there?", I ask, although I already know the answer.

"None of us dares going up", one man explains.

I draw my sword and climb up the stairs.

The staircase leads to a narrow corridor, illuminated by a few torches hanging from the walls. On my left, a wide window overlooks the entrance hall. Straight on, I see a large ebony door.

I cross the corridor and blast the door with a kick.

"Keres!", I shout.

But the room is empty.

Keres' bedroom is large, with red carpeted walls. In the center there is a round bed with a tiger skin for a blanket. There are Egyptian jars, a giant colored marble and a statue of a bear made of some green material.

Also, there are paintings on the walls, framed in gold. The paintings invariably depict a young man fighting monsters and giants, protecting beautiful princesses and enjoying the company and favors of the nymphs of the forest. That must be Lord Keres.

In the paintings he looks very pale, smooth-faced, with dark hair in a bowl cut. His chubby face tries and fails to project confidence, his smile unconvincing. A child in a man's body.

I turn away from the pictures. Along the walls of the room I see several open ivory trunk, all empty. A rectangular window shows a view of the back of the palace. When I get close, I notice something gleaming on the windowsill.

It is a metal lace. A thick rope with knots, tied to the lace, falls through the back wall of the palace all the way down to the floor.

Looking in the dark through the window, I picture the silhouette of the Lord, loaded with treasures, running towards the horizon.

What the hell, it's just money.

I leave the room. On my way to the stairs, I pass by the corridor's window, and see that the whole village of Nephele is waiting in the hall. I see Zeus, Leto, Artemis and Hermes holding hands. And Homer, his father and his mother. And the carpenter. And good old Telemachus. They are all there, waiting for the good news.

I lean on the windowsill for a while until someone notices me. Soon, everyone is silent. They are all looking at me.

"He's gone!", I announce.

And then the men clap, and the women cry and the children jump. And suddenly the crowd is shouting:

"Thasus! Thasus! Thasus! Thasus!"

From the window I can see my reflection on the pool in the middle of the hall: a tall, muscled man with brown beard, wearing a winged golden helmet and an armor, a double-edged sword in his hand.

Just like those old reliefs depicting my father.

XXXIII

I am about to leave the palace when Anaxagoras sees me:
"Are you going home?"
"You bet!", I reply.
"Please tell Zeus that he's delayed with his taxes. Again."
"He didn't pay yet? What's wrong with him?"

Anaxagoras rolls his eyes. He comes from Alexandria, where he was a professor of geometry. I recruited him four months ago, to help me handle the village's economy. He works on economic planning one or two hours per day: the rest of the time Anaxagoras conducts research in mathematics. As soon as I told him that the job didn't carry teaching duties, he accepted the position.

I say goodbye to Anaxagoras and leave the palace.

On my way home, I bump into a group of soldiers practicing with the sword. One of them, a 16-year-old, stops his training to intercept me.

"King Thasus!", he greets.
"Hello, Cadmus. How's it going?"
"The sword is definitely not for me. When will we learn to handle the spear?"
"Uh! That will take time."

Cadmus is disappointed.

"But, hey, cheer up! Starting tomorrow, Artemis will teach you archery. That will give you a rest from the sword."

His eyes shine. "Archery...! I can't wait, king Thasus!"

I leave Cadmus dreaming of gory battles.

King Thasus. I'm still not used to.

When the euphoria ran out, the villagers realized that they still needed a man to run the place. Someone to collect the taxes, repair the roads and protect them from the bandits. After they appointed me king, I started building a small army.

And shortly after, I married Artemis. We don't live in the palace, but in her father's farm, with Zeus, Leto and Hermes. I work in the palace during the morning and help them with the fields in the afternoon.

Everyone calls me Thasus, no one has addressed me otherwise for the last four years. I asked them to call me Thessalus, to no avail. The villagers just stare at me, confused.

"Who is Thessalus?", they ask.

Good question. Who am I, Thessalus or Thasus? I don't know. I still hold very dear memories of my father, teaching me the art of war in an empty ground near our little farm in Tyria. But as of late I have started to recall these childhood scenes from my father's point of view. It is me, and not my father, who instructs young Thessalus in the use of the sword and the spear. It is me who takes Thessalus out for a hunt and swims with him in the lake. At the end of the day, when little Thessalus lies in bed, I tell him stories of gods and heroes, of giant monsters in faraway lands. And I watch his tiny brown eyes glow.

I can now see our farm. Zeus and Leto sit on the porch, under the cool shade. Hermes is chasing the cat. Strangely, Artemis is working in the field. She looks so pretty.

She's six-month pregnant, we're both very excited. If it's a boy, she wants to name him Zeus.

No way. His name will be Thessalus, just like his father.

Hermes is the first to notice me. With a cry, he starts running for a hug. Artemis has stopped her work and smiles at me.

A wife, a family and a kingdom. What more could I wish? Who wouldn't like to be in my sandals?

However, yesterday a very weird thing happened. A man from Iolcus came to the palace. His name was Jason, and he told me that he was organizing an expedition to the East: he wanted to find the fleece of the mythical golden-woolled ram. Jason had heard of my deeds, and he wanted me to join his crew.

Anaxagoras, Artemis, my in-laws and even young Hermes laughed out loud when I told them the story.

But I have spent the whole day turning the idea over in my mind.

Made in the USA
Columbia, SC
11 March 2025